SONNETS TO PARADISE

NIDRA NAIK

Leadstart
INKSTATE

ISBN 978-93-5438-712-8

First published in India 2021 by Leadstart Inkstate
A Division of One Point Six Technologies Pvt Ltd

119-123, 1st Floor, Building J2, B - Wing,
Wadala Truck Terminal, Wadala East,
Mumbai 400022, Maharashtra, INDIA
Phone: +91 969933000
Email: info@leadstartcorp.com
www.leadstartcorp.com

Disclaimer: The views expressed in this book are those of the Author and do not pertain to be held by the Publisher.

Editor: Vaibhav Pathare
Illustration: Shreya Nayak
Cover: R. Maharajan
Layouts: Kshitij Dhawale

To Hyderabad!

To My Friends!

Acknowledgement

Always grateful to my family for letting me be!

CONTENTS

1

WALKING DOWN OR WALKING AWAY

'It's so cold!' I exhaled deeply with a flushed heart and a corroded present. The gushing cold and slithering wind of the west ran down my spine, reminding me of the heartless past and the callous future.

With the temperature plummeting abruptly, I fastened my pace to reach the next bus stop. That was the problem with this English soil, like my life, it was too sudden, stony yet had a warmth to it. The everyday commutation from my office to my place of living had become a rigorous affair, not in terms of physicality but in terms of my mentality.

Sometimes, I am lost at my workplace, messing things up, mishandling clients' requirements, and overtly requesting forgiveness. The senior leadership has been patient so far but not for long I assume. This under-focused character of mine has become a regular trait off-lately. The reason divulged and ramified.

There seemed to be no bus since it had already started snowing, although I had prepared enough still I felt the tough weather. The heavy snowing made the streets sparsely populated, hardly a handful of nomads like me! Unlike yesterday, I decided to walk, knowing that it would not be smooth. But who said life was smooth enough! Looking at the fallen weather, I reconsidered that my idea of walking was not required.

Maybe it was the late 30s that keeps blabbering to me these days. Often, I have found myself on the brink of past glories and a lonely present. The trouble lies in my social skills too! It was long that I had travelled to even London to meet a dear one. Forget taking the flights to India.

There were no buses, which meant I had to walk by. The street lamps were robust, yet getting snowed over. The flickering lights, although dimmer than the regular, providing some air of relief. The side-ways quickly getting filled under the white sheath, the tiny bakeries crying for a regular business loss and shutting down for the day, I meanwhile, walking rampantly like some war-hero, looking at the nature-mystified surroundings, yet getting bothered by my inner-state of being.

There I see my house, a warm little haven in the English land of Rickmansworth, looking regal yet lacking the emotional allurement of a home. A home that had been the warmth of my childhood, the seed of all my secrets, the heart of all my youthful desires. Where Jojo and I were the yardstick of sacrifices and the curiosity of adolescent love. But who knows whether that was love or only the desires of a youth! Mysterious to date.

'Uhh, Mrs Patrick is not in,' I murmured to myself.

Fiddling with my purse, I found the house keys in a rather clumsier way. It was dark, and the keyhole refused to look at me, making it difficult to get through my own place. On getting flustered and irked, I sat at the staircase which thankfully had a hood on top of it, protecting me from the snow and the frustration of not being able to get inside of my house. The mobile phone had run out of battery, making it difficult to even consider a call.

The fatigue of the everyday journey to work and the depression of the weather made my eyelids heavier, making me groggy, and finally resting my head on the edge of the main door.

The creaking of the front gate, with a tall dark figure, woke me up. The figure stood there, unmoved at the threshold of the gate, creating panic issues within me. Was he a murderer, a rapist, a ghost or just an illusion! I sat still too. My anticipation was pacing with my racing heartbeat. It was an awry evening for sure, maybe it was the last day of my life, my lonely life.

Across the gate, I could partially see him, with a long trench coat and a hat of some sort. He was slightly awkward in his figure, trying to avoid the snowfall on his attire that seemed a waste to this weather. His brawny arms, constantly fidgeting with the front of his hat, maybe trying to get rid of this horrendous weather. With each passing second, he seemed to be in some sort of restlessness, itching his left foot with his right. His gaze often changed direction, but nothing seems to catch his steady attention. Few moments of watching him made me realize that he was more into himself, his anxiety to protect from this awful weather! It brought in some relief to me at first but also a sentiment of deflation since there was no man of that sort in my life to this day. This absurdly dark shadow mirrored my life's flaws and prejudices, snapping at my withering age and single self.

Some vicious nerve in me instigated me to talk to this man, help him out in a hopeless surrounding, where the graves had literally taken over the Sun.

I plodded my body up, taking the support of the doorway staircase's railing. Fixing my eyes on the tall-unknown man, I happened to drop my belongings with a thud sound. The undesirable sound got vaporised in the hissing sound of the snow. I placed my foot towards the main gate where the figure was almost like a non-representation of a civilised society. He seemed completely engrossed in his oddities, without bothering much about the woman in the background. There was a streak of courage in me that poked me to understand his ask. Somehow, I had a feeling that he was in frantic search of something, something of emotional value, maybe.

'Mister,'

His back of the body suddenly jerked up by my calling. He seemed conscious, petrified, and tried hiding his shadowy face in the blind night of the snow. By this time, I was almost wet, feeling nature's coldest form taking over my partial-old self.

I again tried being calm, and this time placed my palms on his shoulders as if we were long-lost friends in need of each other. He turned into a statue, with no movement, giving me a slight jolt of surprise. What kind of man was he who apparently melted into his shell by a mere touch of a woman?

This thought evaporated and no sooner than the tall-unknown man with the courage of a prey, turned his face towards me. The dense fall of the snow made it impossible to look at him. His voice, as if blurred with lack of power and anxiety, meekly, 'help!'

And alas! He thumped onto the pebbled pathway right in front of my eyes, in this terribly cold weather of Rickmansworth. I stood still for some time as if being indecisive of my future movement. He was not tiny, not even feather-light for me to pick him and just dump him somewhere. The snow was turning harsher, like a wicked witch's spell. I had to think fast and act faster.

'Ah…Mrs Patrick, thank God, you are here!' I cried out of exasperation.

'Madame, you alright?'

'Not exactly, help me!'

'Let me unlock the house doors for you.'

'Give me a few minutes here, let me understand what to do here.'

Mrs Patrick was the torchbearer in my life. In this soil of the lesser-known, she stood by me whenever I needed her the most. She's the calmest person who I can be with, a friend indeed, a sister of laugh and a mother of patience to me.

She was the housekeeper, and I was the namesake home-keeper. I met her 3 years back, when I was clinically depressed and had the least motivation to survive. I met her at a sobriety centre and life seemed bright post that. She was a sturdy woman, a mountaineer herself with a love story that could turn into a great book after Love in the Time of Cholera!

Tall, pale, fair, knowledgeable, courageous, kind, and friendly were a few attributes that I can relate to her. She wore a thick black frame with an English bun, mostly to be found in trousers and shirts! Uncommonly in frocks! She pushed me ahead to live, to take charge of everything that was fragmented, and saw in me a hopeful tinge that my hopeless heart could not.

My inane mind tried pulling the stranger from his structured position. He had passed out, in front of my doorway, where nobody ever stood, ever came for help or anything of humane for that matter.

'Huh,' I gasped. Yet the energy to be the saviour didn't stop, the overwhelming desire to keep this man out of unconsciousness didn't wither. With the help of Mrs Patrick, I could cross the doorway corridor and put this man in place next to my hallway's fireplace. It was tiring; to drag a man this stout and tall! He lay like a stone, cold and uncared; his face gloomy, melancholic; his clothes extremely worn-out, outdated, soaked in this troublesome weather, but his hands were soft, pulpy like that of a child, a young man in teens. It was extraordinary since he had a huge build, maybe 6 feet if taped. His looks were not mesmerising, at least not in this failed condition. The dishevelled self of him infused sympathy in my heart. He looked like the total case of longed and lost!

This stormy night, sitting by his side and watching his disregarded figure, struck me that maybe one day I might end up in solitude, being the sole reaper of it. I hushed away those thoughts, which came haunting frequently to me these days. The fireplace was dimmer and my eyelids heavier, carrying the blotch of the past. The fatigue of the day and Mrs Patrick's clear soup tricked my mind to rest finally.

Wham! Thud! Huh! As if in my dreams, I was trying to escape from a dungeon, dark and literally dingy. I woke up getting disturbed, my heart mulled and beating fast as if I was victimised in an island of known. The sheer lace curtains looked familiar, so did the antique neoclassical window, the thatched Portuguese angular roof, with a solid old fan, a creaky bed, a two-legged worn-out stool, a dim lamp-shed by the wobbly small door, a mosaic floor and a breathing slim body!

Did I time travel! I murmured to myself. I pinched my skin thrice, as they show in movies, to verify whether in dreams, strangely, I wasn't. I tried getting up from the bed, my legs felt sedated, my body fatigued by some rigorous activity, the left side of my neck burning with probably a rash, my heart racing, the hair dishevelled, breasts tighter, and that sudden walk giving a crampy pain in my groin. The place felt so familiar but not this pain; I wanted to relieve myself. Looking for the restroom, I unlatched the wobbly door with the utmost care, not wanting to disturb the figure on the bed. Stepping out of the room, I looked at a naïve old world. The corniced exterior and the typical inwardly built house. Numbness surrounded my cognitive-ability, but I finally found the restroom at the posterior end of the house.

The mouth of the genital burnt, giving it a slight itch. It scared me of an infection. I tried to ignore my negations. Finishing my business, I loyally returned to that same room. The slim figure seemed to be that of a young man, facing his half bare back towards the door where I stood. I approached the bed, the entire room now lighted by the break of dawn. Something urged me to place my hands to caress his back, some strong undercurrent of emotion. The touch of his back, as if not too new to me. It gave me a certain level of emotional belongingness, to this person lying so deep in sleep. I figured out a few moles on his back, some too dark and prominent, other small in its texture. His skin was soft, not that of a body-builder, not too muscular, a little boyish. He could be called a typical coastal skin-toned since he was neither too dark nor too fair, let's say wheat like!

My mind seemed to be playful, I breathed seductively next to the back of his ear, his sleep got perturbed. It made me giggle, forgetting about the streak of pain in my private area. The figure abruptly changed his sides, as if unlocking himself to me, his identity to me!

'Whispering next to my ears has become your habit, girl!'

His hands were stretched across my chest, holding my set of fingers loosely. His smile was sheepish, creating a depression on his chin, the face a little bony, lack of facial flesh, nose sharper at the tip, carrying a mole of irritation on it.

'Leave me! You common man, you coastal boy,' I said with a smirk, trying to win the tussle between the fingers.

'After last night, no chance, my girl,' his voice crossed between a bass and a guitar, meaning no gravity.

'I can give you a good fight. You bet?'

'I am so sure sweetheart that you can…but will I let you?' he said holding my hands a little tighter this time, bringing his lean body's weight over mine, exposing his nude limbs and brushing his genitals against mine, his lips wanting to seize mine playfully.

'Love has its limitations set
Sometimes to Exclusivity
And at times to Adherence...
The stroke of your body can I mutter
Has fallen for this bodily pleasure
Fusion of lust, longing & a lot of manly splatter
Beware, my lover, there are convulsions
In the lanes that you seek for so-called Godly redemption'

As if I was watching me, me with the boy of lost times, a time when the Sun shone on our heads, the rain gods waited for our approval, the stars twinkled with the brush of our hands, and the sky turned violet with the meeting of our eyes. The times that were a gone era, no more around me; a time that was the yesteryears of Jojo and me humming the strings of Steve Wonder's classic, 'I just call to say…' in a place that all lovers had once wanted their lives at, a place that was laid-back, with mesmerising evenings and illusionary sea waves. Goa, the place where it had all begun!

2

Poetry in Goa

'Leave me, asshole, get your hands off me, you…uh,' the fallen yelled.

The glistening knob of the stove pricked my hand, there was a piercing thin and tiny metal protruding from it. I bled by the fallen man's distressful call. Having offered him a helpful hand demanded me to be overly sensitive and compassionate. I ran for him.

Mrs Patrick saw me retreating to the living room. She was patting the hugely built man. There was a comic scene being replicated from some Laurel-Hardy movie, where a woman house-keeper was consoling a giant metamorphosis of life! Ridiculous yet etched by the tragedy that life puts us…

'O dear, let me give you a hand,' I said panicking.

'His torso is heavier than his limbs, uhhh,' cried Mrs Patrick.

'Never mind, some men are built stout and others not,'

'O these men, Nayan, drive women crazy, sometimes with their love, passion and at others, with their sorrows and atrocities.'

'Rightly said.'

The rugged huge man was put to sub-consciousness by his wounds and depression. We just caressed his head.

I must admit that he was not the ignorable type, something about his presence was striking, very attractive. He was unconventional, for whichever reasons maybe! His crow-feet wrinkles and worry lines talked about his dragging struggle and experiences. He seemed to be a man of valour, yet seeking shelter, some homeliness, that probably was fissured in his long-dusted journey. Mesmerised by my capability of being an observant, I looked at his wrists. The handcuffs of his sleeves were taken off, depicting slight dirt on the edges of the cuff. The wrist was twice my size, foretelling his labour-like history, highlighting points of pain and treason. His life, yet confirming him holding onto some positivity.

Nursing him that night didn't bring in any resemblance of this man with Jojo! Neither in the physicality, cannot presume behaviour dissimilarities now though! I was waiting for the weird and disturbing night to end. I somehow wanted to discover this man's truth, share his distress, and make him feel comfortable. His presence as if intimidating my loneliness.

I fell asleep by the fireplace, next to this hugely built man.

'Nayan, wake-up!' cried Mrs Patrick in weariness.

'What happened?'

'That man, that huge man, injured one, is no longer to be found!'

'Whoa!!!'

'Yes, Nayan!'

While taking a shower, ironing my clothes, fixing my hair, doing my eyes, and dressing for the day, I followed the unfollowed path of the stranger. Thinking about the inconclusive happenings in his life, his tragic situation, although stoic presence. Memories can be some messy affairs at times, at least in case of me.

The roads, because of the previous nights' heavy snowfall, were damp and chilly, which was a routine in a fluctuating place like

Rickmansworth. It would not be surprising if while retreating from my workplace, the temperatures would rise to 19 degrees! Learning about this man seemed to be my curiosity! His thankless outgoing from my haven was not a little but a wholesome disturbance. I had started expecting even without knowing him. Somehow, I had a feeling that we had a connection!

'Hey, Nayan! You're early to work today!'

'Hey, Sam! I am glad about it!'

After consecutive failures of not reaching office on time, today was a celebratory day. It seemed my life was disrupting misshapenness, but how?

'The fall it was, a previous night,
It bought a man, with brooding dark no light,
My fate disrupted his struggling path, it seems,
Our faces never met in such tenacity,

He brought with him, my memories old,
Flashing with colourful youth and brimming gold,
I teleported to the land that was once a story,
Met an old pal in romantic scenery!'

I typed while the train was halting at each sub-station, looking outside the glass-window that had droplets of fog, shimmering like some silver dust, yet disappearing as the typical nature of water droplets. Absurdly, my mind was seeking romance with the mundane things of life. Joyously or so, I had suddenly started being an optimist's tail, if not the head!

It was six in the evening, the weather took a magical turn, the flowy drapes dancing to the tune of the faint strings, I was nervous, fidgeting with my wrist-watch, sometimes pulling the band and at the other, raising the nape of my neck, twisting and turning to each side, cleaning my glasses, patting my square jaw-line, massaging my forehead, popping my knuckles, curling my tresses, adjusting the shift of my skirt, crossing my legs and yet not able to find the boy who had busted the question of this year-let's move in together!'

'Ladies & Gentlemen, presenting to you, Calangute's upcoming musicians, The Strummers!' I angled my face to the elevated dais and waited for the guitarists to take the stage. The show started with slightly organized fireworks, people around me applauded for it was one of the local's favourite bands, performing on such a huge platform- at the Goa Institute of Management youth festival. My eyes were set on the stage, I could see all the musicians and vocalists making impressive entries onto the stage but I seldom found the slim guy who very radically wanted to spend time with me. Yes, a two-syllabled named local boy, Jojo, who looked only 15 years of age, proposed to me in the most vehement way possible, as if my entire existence was at his command! While doing so, he rarely cared for the surroundings, his parents' notions, all he had in his childish round eyes, was affability and on his tiny sharp nose, steadfastness, which was quite non-bearing!

The prelude was done, and the main lead had already started voicing out his superbly practiced songs, the interlude was directed by amazing music, a kick-ass strumming, but hello, the ferocious being with a body of an itsy insect was not to be found-liar!

There was a sudden pause in the middle of the song, the rock-beats became softer, the rock-solid became the starry-melody, a bit of a romantic if I'd admit- with the appearance of the two-syllabled guy!

#F sharp and #Dm with an up-down strumming of #C Major and #Am chords, he strummed so beautifully that the evening was crowned for him!

The lead singer sang, rather something familiar;

'O girl of the Mud, meet me, I am a guy of the Sand!
O girl of the Floods, meet me, I am a guy of the Storm!
Hmmmm….OOOOO…..Yayyyy….'

The lead singer was joined by this lean local boy, taking the stanza's notes to a higher range

'My heart stopped for your complexion, a tone that only angels possess,
Crazy heart it is, you know since you know the lightning between two roses.'

The strumming paused and the focus light was on this crazy fellow, who called out loudly, 'Naads, trust me, please!' And went ahead with the craziest lines ever!

'Alongside the beaches of Margao, where no man has dared love but hate,

By the seashore of Colva, where no seagulls but glow-worms have spread their fate,

I promise, O Nayan, my new-found muse,

I will immerse in your almond-eyes,

With all senses, soul and energy fuse,

Making love to you is all I desire,

No music is worth it, without you being there!'

'O girl of the Mud, meet me, I am a guy of the Sand!

O girl of the Floods, meet me, I am a guy of the Storm!

Hmmmm....OOOOO.....Yayyyy....'

'Thud!' my heart sounded as if the blood pumping was public. My mind, as if still translating the ludicrous boy's silly act and my body, losing all the five chakras attained through steady wellbeing of yoga!

'How dare he! Silly, he! Preposterous act!' my mind shouted.

I carefully stood up from my firm stance of ignorance. Taking a deep breath, I made my way through the once organized row of chairs, to the campus hostel where instead I was engulfed by my space, my privacy and no interference.

By getting admitted to this great institute, I recollected that super proud forehead of my parents, and the cultural diversity that I was born into. It was no achievement that I had been offered a role in one of the reputed banks out here, only to be confronted by this guy's hideous deed of outraging my modesty, my name, out there in public, for his so-called desire, spelled in an opportunist way called 'LUST!'

'Youth, they say, is coated.

Coated with compassion and innocence

With unreserved boundaries of Love,

Where distance seldom falls prey
When all colour of the skin is syrupy
When all physicality of the body
Is united by just one word, 'Soulfulness!'

Youth, they say, is Freedom,
Freedom to express the sweetest things of life…'

I clicked my pen in irritation. My feelings were in disdain, maybe any other girl in my place would have loved the craziness that Jojo had displayed, his profound youthful charm would have made any girl fall for his music, his style, his boyish looks, but just any other girl not me!

To my dismayed heart, my space and aspirations took priority in this place of competition. Love was a far-flung idea, and lust was just not the cup of tea that I wanted to dip my tongue into. However, Jojo had used my private dialogues to pen his song, which took my heart further away from him.

3

Infused with Life

My brain was a little heavier, absurd as if I was stuck in the after-concert at Goa! Taking that huge baggage off was almost impossible, it seemed to me. I thought of diverting my focus to the non-expected activities.

'Yoga! The key to peaceful living. I should be back on track with it,' I said to myself.

After a long time, I felt my senses alive and functioning. I watched many online episodes- of power yoga, for reducing weight, for dealing with critical diseases, for reviving the positive thoughts, for junking the rigid mind and body, for adapting to the world of not expecting and so much more.

A full month passed by, and I evolved from a troublesome personality to a charismatic one. My peers were astounded, and so were the managers. My boss, as if had almost given up on me, found in me a sense of drive. I sensed that everything was connected, connected to that hugely built man. But not much was seen of him after that night. His incoming was, as if a boon, a blessing to my ruined, disputed life.

Life was injected to my so-called life in a greater way, in a way that few months flew by! I looked as rejuvenated as my Goa days. It wouldn't be wrong to address myself as a beautiful lady since I was turning to my old self. My life was returning to bounce me up, to pep me up and all after meeting that stout man.

Deciding to drive to the weekly market at Volde's crossing didn't give me a second mind about not having driven for the past so many months. However, I used to be an ace driver, my father taught me driving the car, calling it to be a mere machine created by none other than intelligent humans like us!

'Driving a car shouldn't give you cold feet, it shouldn't control you! Your mind is nothing but a genius, you are the creator of everything around you. Go ahead Buli, drive it, race it!'

And that's what my father had said to me while I was shaking in nervousness by this engine's stuttering sound. It was back in Puri where I'd learnt to drive a car. I had taken up driving lessons again when I was working in London. A dear friend had forcibly enrolled my name in the monthly lessons for an international license.

Mrs Patrick, my only family member in the UK, had brought two of her adopted dogs named Elsa and Nelsa. They were a few of the cutest beings that I had come across in recent times. Elsa was super-active, was ready to gobble every pebble given to her but Nelsa was sober. A gentleman, he would wait for his turn, a sincere and diligent dog. Both of them were English Foxhounds, Elsa was completely white, and Nelsa was a combination of lemon and white. I'd very recently discovered this side of me, getting invigorated, fascinated by animals. Communicating with them, feeling their energy, their positive vibes with introducing these two lively beings. And I was thankful to Mrs Patrick.

An army of us marched through the weekly market. Mrs Patrick, trying her best commands to manage the pets. She excused herself to the nearby crockery store, where she wanted to bring something for the house. I was thrilled to be a part of this energetic crowd that didn't stop until their wallets shed the pounds. Locating my favourite snack bar, Pete's Patisserie, I wished to stop by and eat some of my delightful pastries- corn and cheese! Looking around the surrounding, the day seemed bright, sunny, with no news of the rain or the dreadful snow.

Rickmansworth weather was as unpredictable as a young bride's heart. It could turn hues. Maybe for later today was a day to be cheerful about, enjoy the company of Elsa and Nelsa, help Mrs Patrick in finding her type of luscious green vegetables, mighty fruits of heaven, as she keeps describing. Today was the day to celebrate life and living that I had somewhere missed in these years of separation.

'To Love is divine
To find one is finding heavens

Looking for Love is to seek truth
Truth that at times takes ages

Who cares for the ticking clock?
As long as my seeking is strong

Wait a minute, did I just see that
That streak of temptation in your once naïve heart

Temptation is the devil that snaps at Love
Love has this test to pass
To cripple down or to stay surmount!'

'Would you go out on a date with me?'

'You! Of all people in this scenic place,' I said while having second thoughts on refusing him.

'Yes, in this place. With me, this average lean guy, who can give you nothing but memories to cherish, so much that when you are in disgust, and out of this nature's basket, you recoup by these beautiful memories.'

'You quote this restlessness in you as good memories! I pity you!'

'Hmmm…and you quote your attraction with this fake disgust.'

There was silence in that small shack. It was a Sunday afternoon, he looked at my almond eyes through my heavily rimmed glasses that

I was so fond of; my eyes that were trying to look at every corner of the shack and outside, at the silvery beach other than his face, moreover his eyes. Because my heart knew those child-like eyes were my weakness, a reflection of my forsaken mind.

'I don't date men who are younger than me!'

'Don't contradict yourself, Naads.'

'My name is better than what you have manipulated it for, it's Nayantara,' I said with a tone of anger.

'Please excuse me for that Naads, but I feel I have nicknamed you for reasons so obvious, you are my likeness, and when you call me young, I feel great, please don't infuse this feeling of mine with man-made boundaries, let the boundaries limit the regular mind, not an irregular guy like me. Age as they say is the math. Man has created to drum its logical intelligence, math is more useful in science, and not in building relationships, maybe in building huge ships!'

I, although was immersed in his poetic monologues but thought this was utterly vain, too impractical, I hail from the East, where the culture with the West is as different as the Sun and the Moon. I am a believer. He is an atheist. He is a Goan. I am an Odia. I am a Hindu. He's a Catholic. I am 22 and he is hardly 19!

'Tell me your problem?' he asked surely

'You, your caste, your region, your age, this difference… everything associated with you is a problem!'

'You sound like an extremist! Wohooo!' he exclaimed.

'If that's what you think, so be it!' I paid my share and was preparing to leave the place when he started singing out of the blue!

'My Ignorant Love…
Let me take you inside the fathomless ocean
Where all boundaries collapse, where all math fails

My Ignorant Love…
Let me fly you above the Nimbus, the Stratus and the Cumulus
Where all merge into a vastness of One, Ours & Us

My Ignorant Love…
Let me carry you across the globe, the earth and the trees
Where creatures who breath have no rule, no math to tie them

My Ignorant Love…My Naads…just let me.'

I was infuriated with anger and exasperation, where all my rhetorical sense was missing, all my sensibility was disoriented, I left for my hostel, my pragmatic residence, where everything made sense and where everything was calculated mindfully.

4

DISCOVERY OF MY SCRAPS

Somehow, I could track the biggest musings of all times, my poems, penned when I was in college. School ones were at my home, in India, handwritten. But my old email inbox had these 'over-the-top' romantic poetries that I had once scribbled in the hope of a dream-like love story, a dream-boy, maybe a man!

Through those poems of bondage free love, I discovered that I had a brighter side of brilliance in me; that exposure of thoughts in the beams of the luscious country-side of Margao; the purity of romance intriguing my soul and the mention of Jojo in most of them created a rather special bond. Those days, if I may describe them, were the most colourful days of my life. Just to realize it today that romance is, but an imagined order of our preconceived ideas about love. Romance doesn't exist. It's created. Created sometimes by the most fantastic minds! And higher than romance is philosophy!

A tear rolled down my cheek, I was not even in my conscious state of mind to acknowledge that I was weeping, which had become too rare of me. But as if heaven shone on me, those words of love, the feelings of elation, the by-lanes of Panjim, Margao, and the little rented hut, were as if my identification, my best direction that I could have ever taken.

I turned off the computer as I was full of old dilapidated thoughts, which made no sense today. However, the inspiration for the poems brought back a lot of old memories.

'Rather, I should cook some noodles in hot garlic sauce,' I assured myself of some great treat if not romance.

Mrs Patrick was out as she was also working as a gardening expert at a city nursery and supervised manoeuvring the garden of the rich Italian lady, who lived at the corner of the street by the street-lamppost. She was a certified gardener from the Snopian School of Art & Culture. The gothic Italian style mostly inspired her work. And to mention that she was a genuine artist on that front.

'A mountaineer, a gardener, a caretaker and what else…' I murmured as the noodle soup did wonders to my poetic appetite. The poems were so relevantly placed. It talked about love, friendship, nature, desire, kindness, and in every piece written in those days, he was an inspiration. Like I was in most of his songs, written back then. When you are in love, it doesn't matter how divided is the geography, all that matters is how united your souls are, your hearts are! And this feeling of love is not full of longing but is filled with adoration and blessings. I now realize that one doesn't have to be with each other to love, one doesn't have to make love regularly to be in love, one doesn't have to hold things tight to show love and one doesn't have to be full of wants to shower love! You can love the most distanced person with the utmost rigor and joy.

The Hotel Christmas Tree was almost 10 kms away from my institution. It was the last exam of my second semester, Retail Marketing, and my joyous heart had no limits of exaggerating happiness. It would be summers and internship season at home, back to basic, back to where I belong for two long months! It exhilarated me for reasons so obvious. I will go back to my hometown, Puri, and spend two months at a stretch after the demanding nature of management studies. The plan was made but as usual the two-syllabled guy interfered in my regular course of life since he had already declared himself to be irregular.

'Uhh...arrrghhh! I don't want to meet him since I can hardly stand him. He's an overconfident, boastful Catholic guy, Reena,' I said while dumping my college bag on the bed and slumping on it!

'The approach to your case study is quite simple. Do not attend the musical! I mean the event. Although I conducted a SWOT to your thrills and it turns out that if you go there, you have more opportunities than threat, you will showcase more strength than weakness,' said Reena.

'But you just asked me not to attend it!'

'I did so. I agree. But you know in management there is always a contingent approach, similarly, when I analysed the situation, I found that there's no harm in attending that event,' said she with a smirk.

Alas! I got dressed in a red skater frock, the hem was just below the knee, tight at my waist, the sleeves stopped right at my elbows with no embellishments or glitters, solid red dress it was. I was thankful to my creators for having given me an hourglass figure. A little light at the top and a little heavier at the bottom, but the landscaping at the middle was exactly the one that any woman would die for- my love handles were the best, nonetheless attractive. Reena had complimented me once! She was persistent in saying that my not so fair, wheat-like complexion added magical flavour to earthy coloured clothes, today it was red! On the contrary, I resembled a Christmas tree!

Reena was a little tom-boyish but straight, had short hair, ending at the nape, and was always seen in a pair of jeans and a statement t-shirt, as per her mood. Wore sneakers, and sported a big dial watch, although her face was absolutely contradictory to her dressing style. She was a gorgeous looking female in full denial. Her eyes were big in comparison to her Russian nose and tiny lips. She wore a geeky, brown framed spectacle that often hid her beautiful eyes. She denied her sexy existence. Defied all gravity of lust. In a nutshell, she was an extraordinary college mate. Just the one you need to hang out with!

She was not a local of Goa but had a few caring relatives, who had gifted her a two-wheeler for an easy commutation. And I was most of the time her companion. That evening, she drove straight ten kilometers to drop me off at the Hotel Christmas Tree! The musical was at 5:30 pm and I was there thirty minutes before the program. The hotel was more of a southern Goa elaborative house, which emanated from the Portuguese extravagance in the place. It was beautiful! Not too huge but full of beauty. The theme was fire and peace, every lady was dressed in either white, off-white, or red. Men were mostly in whites. I had an invitation, Jojo had dropped in at my hostel's reception with a note that said:

> *'With every beat of my heart, I will strum the chord of the guitar,*
> *With every exhale of your breath, I will wait at the threshold tonight,*
> *Let fire and peace unite…will play for you under the starry night!*
> *-The lean two-syllabled guy!'*

'Nayantara, here is your special place,' said one of the hotel attendants that surprised me. I very reluctantly sat at the second row of round tables that held a tiny flower vase, a few tiny bottles of water, an off-white satin cloth to cover the plastic facade of the table. It was surrounded by four chairs and I could sit in the so-called special place, which I truly didn't register much, as every place had almost a nice view of the small dais.

Drums, Electric Keyboard, Saxophone, Electric Guitar, Bass Guitar, Cajon, Cello and Tambourine and maybe harmonica! I knew all the names since once by coincidence when I had met Jojo, he had introduced me to all the musical instruments and he knew almost all of them. At the tender age of six, he had exhaled music with the harmonica, beaten usually by his dad to be dedicated to learning it, but he had said that he was too sluggish and laid back. Nevertheless, his negligent attitude had taught him almost all the string instruments, synthesizer, and Cajon! I couldn't believe him unless I had actually heard him play a few. It was impressive, at 18, he could play the world of instruments and still wore it like a t-shirt. He was casually so passionate about music, it sometimes surprised me. And he had also confessed that the only thing lacking in his life was an inspiration!

The band started with Simon & Garfunkel's famous folk rock when the crowd cheered with excitement and nostalgia. Jojo was on Cello, this time, he swept my senses off as if I saw a dream being sequenced, and while all this was happening, he didn't look at me at all while performing. The evening was ending with musicians speaking something about their lives, dedication, struggle, but Jojo kept quiet, uttered nothing, which was a little absurd. He was a boy who wouldn't fail or limit his heart's say, anywhere, he could be boastful about his love for music, given at any point of time. But today he was different, another side of him, rather grave which was very disturbing. But the question that bothered me was very unusual. Why was his indifference, a botheration to me!!!

5

THE YOUNG COUPLING

After a couple of months of frantically looking for the man who had rotated the compass of my life, changed my outlook, my quality of living; had perpetually disappeared, poof into thin air! He was never to be seen, heard, or found! I had enquired in the District Council's office at odd hours of last Saturday, with just Mrs Patricks' reference. Stoic appearance, gloomy presence, six feet tall, heavy built, hammered expressions and a pained face, with a sharp nose, not to forget the high raised hairline on the forehead, and dark skin tone that defined the nameless man, who had been at the door of my fate by chance, and even without his knowledge had invariably given me with some yesteryears memories and poems, recreating my stagnant life, spelling a charm on my dead self. The man who was pinned down by his own disaster, to a great extent injured, had by the struck of the clock, altered me invariably to a life that I could now die for. His presence was divine, he was significant to my existence! The connection is undefined, yet strong!

Sincerely, I wanted to show him my gratitude, to narrate to him what a regeneration he had injected in me, what his unconsciousness had zoned me into! I just wanted to take care of him, understand his needs, his struggling past, the reason for his injuries, external and internal, mend him, provide support and do things that I couldn't do for Jojo!

'Recipe of Love begins with swift romance,
Sometimes with dreamy eyes and at times with vibrant instance,

When Love stricken ones' ogle,
It has oozing sentiments tingle,

Wee hours' wants and indefinite expectations,
Countless fantasies with mesmerized annotations,

O those eyes that do the wonders,
Piercing my heart with some unknown flavours,

The recipe of Love lies in holding onto your favourite emotions,
And also freeing it when in full adoration!'

Nature was at its best mood, sometimes thundering and parting across clouds, the incessant rain didn't stop, but it stopped my human heart. The musical was followed by a mixture of waltz and tango, not limiting itself to the heavy drizzle. Jojo's upcoming act of romance was as classy as his passion for music. I was sceptical and nervous. The differences popping in and out of my sight, my God and his Heaven dashing with religious barriers! The math encircling my vision, and I, feeling giddy and my thoughts drifting away to his love and compassion, making me stranded in the house-full of strangers.

Holding my dangling hands, he pulled me into the swarm of people busy in their affairs. With heroic guts, he put his hands around my waist without seeking my permission. His breathing is full of romance, but his eyes sadder than the regular days.

'I am a poor dancer, two left feet,' I said, and he whispered into my ears to trust him on this!

'Not sure to trust you,' I said with a tinge of arrogance.

'Sorry to disappoint you, but you already have. You are just not into acceptance!'

I looked at him a little surprised, a little magical since he professed what I wouldn't ever have! In true sense, an egoistic, ram-headed creature I was. Flooding pragmatism into the best of moments of life!

He forcibly pulled me closer towards him, his grip growing firmer around my waist, his round childlike eyes set on mine, losing no focus! The air turning warmer, his fingers moving in sync with the musical notes, from my waist towards the nape of my neck. I was totally captivated by his act, my mind asking him to release me but his musings still holding me back. Not trying to nullify the evening, I wanted to lose control over my pragmatic mind for once, since every passing second with him rolled like a love-filled memory. The more I tried to drift away, the closer I was drawn. Amid such ambience, I placed my arms on his shoulders, a little roughly than he would have expected. He was caught by a little shock since my impulsiveness was not something that he must have anticipated. I placed my slender palms on the back of his neck, closed my eyes dramatically, and when the entire world was revolving around us, I placed my lips on his…

It was then when the nightfall was silent, we couldn't hear the people chattering, or the attendants chuckling, neither could we feel the water falling on us and drenching us entirely, the oceans creating a thunderous sound, the clouds bursting to whatever decibel, nor did we realize that we were blending into something perpetual, something forever, some knotted affair unlimited to social barriers. That minute, Jojo had taken me out of that place, to some secluded corner of his land, I just followed him wherever his footsteps marched. Pushing me to a damp wall of something, he had asked me to trust him.

His hands held the little of my back, pressing it a little harder than I would have imagined, his long fingers caressing my torso, and that tingling sensation creating thousands of more vibrations in my body. He had kissed too passionately that night, one of its kind, where there was no technique of perfection but strength of compassion. That kiss, contracted she in me, till today, letting me be a little desperate of what I have been missing in all these years.

6

JOJO'S STORY

'His hands, does much more than playing strings,

His hands, slender, warm and full of zing,

His hands, with magical long fingers, is no less than a ping,

His hands, if held tight, allows the travel of world and also the wild,

His hands, if holds you tight, sweeping off the ground is eased like a child,

His hands, around you, are like injecting lost love life,

His hands, with meagre touch, spilling melody,

His hands, amusing, admirable and sexy, just not around anymore!

His hands, not around… anymore!'

Penning down the last lines of the poem made me quiet, as if not wanting to let go of those memories, those lovely ones! In the meantime, the afternoon of Saturday was as sluggish as the snails trying to cross the shore-line. I rested my head on the study table and looked outside the apartment's tiny window that held the entire world's empathy, emotion, and life externally. Looking through that window, I was trying to live my previous days again, yet again, with more vigour, less complains, more love, and less pragmatism.

Lost in translating what could have been bettered back then, I remembered something that Jojo had always believed in doing…not worrying about a situation that was not under his control- letting it go, thinking like a chain-free animal, running wild into the oceans, vrooming zig-zag on his bike, and picking up any musical instruments and playing it like any mundane work! He was distinct and so were his ways of looking at things!

But that day Jojo was reserved. He wanted to meet me at the fort's rear end in the scorching summer of April, just a week before I was about to begin my summer internship. I, although in denial of my state of heart, was already involved with him in all human aspects possible, hence overlooking his request was simply out of question. I had to meet him.

Reaching at the Aguada fort, sharp at 5 in the evening, was one of the most intriguing brushes with Jojo's tryst with life. He was not himself for sure; I remember the rendezvous so vividly! He stood there, facing the endless horizon, wearing a solid white shirt with khakhi shorts, his lean body slouching on the walls of the fort, and his expressions wearisome about the purpose of his existence.

'You don't look alright,' I said, patting on his shoulders.

He chuckled, his wrinkles not matching the expressions of his eyes. 'I am delighted that you can read me so well! Nobody cared all this while but you!' and held my hands tight.

'…and I am listening.'

'Do you mind giving me a head massage?'

'Huh? Massage!' I said in shock.

'Yeah, you mind?'

I looked at him minutely, his eyes demanding it with brimming melancholy. Giving in to his request, I said, 'Why not!'

We sat on the red solid rock, partially shadowed by the wall from the piercing Sun of the humid land. There were few passers-by, who must have thought, how insanely lost we were! He placed his handkerchief beneath my knees, since I was kneeling, readying myself for this gentle request of him, not wanting to turn him down, and also showing my warmer side to him.

'Ahhh, Naads, listen, I earn nine thousand bucks in a month by playing instruments with the band, plus I am a tutor to four pupils. They learn acoustic guitar and violin, also the keyboard. My mother is a teacher of music in the St. Holy Cross school, imparting music ever since I remember. She is an industrious woman, never seen her relaxing. If not in the school, she bakes cakes for weddings or for small birthday parties, although there is no typical confectionary that we own…you know for neighbours, relatives, friends, friends of friends… it runs by word of mouth. She makes a reasonable sum of money that allows us to lead a non-luxurious life but with certain ease and comfort. Thankfully, we are putting up at my grandfather's place, with no rent to dispose at the beginning of a month. It's like our own residence, old yet with a sober charm. I will be a graduate in Fine Arts within a year and a half and then grab a full-time job.'

'How about your father, you hardly speak about him?'

'Umm…he's hardly a part of our lives, he never took any pride in us, never believed in owning me, as if I was not his part.'

'But, didn't he teach you music?'

'He did, initial days of my childhood, my playful days. In my wonder days, I was beaten up badly to learn instruments. I had developed a hatred towards music. He would order me to kneel and play the violin for the Church concerts. I did it out of fear, fear of getting thrashed by him. Being a single child didn't rejuvenate my sense of right. I was, regularly treated as an orphan, my mom staying away for work most of the time. I didn't understand this dislike that he carried for me. He said that I was born not from the seed of love but the thorns of sin.'

A tear rolled down his eyes, my fingers stopped twirling around his eyes. I felt his emotions rolled in the salty water. Relaxing my knees, I sat next to him, holding his long, slender fingers.

'Did he like your mom?'

'Difficult to answer that. Sometimes he adored her spirit of survival, the way she took her responsibilities, and the rest of the time, he made her slog like his slave, asking her for many unreasonable favours. Asking her to cook him mutton, when only fish was available at home. Waking her up in the middle of the night to serve him a peg of whisky, warning her that if her services are not up to the standards, he will divert himself to another anglicised beauty. At times, even slapping her blue-black when the dishes were not done before bed! Gaining sadistic pleasure to see her weep.'

'Ohhh that's so horrible! I am so sorry for these anomalies you have been through.'

He looked at me intensely and cupped my cheeks and said, 'I bring with me abnormalities and irregularities, like crude mountains and the meandering waters, but it's true that with you by my side, these irregularities fuse into something exuberant, something deep and something charming. I am so charmed by you, your presence, Naads! I am glad that Jesus brought you into my dull life.'

'Thank you,' I said with a sheepish smile.

'I thank you and the Lord!'

'Where's your father, now?'

'Death has him now! A tyrannical father and a useless husband! Even music couldn't save him from his dirty drinking. Once he had created theatrical nonsense at the altar of St. Mary's Cathedral, the crowd started pelting him with pebbles. My maternal Uncle who is an office-bearer at the Church had saved him. He had bled profusely, and so had my mother in disgrace!'

He started sobbing, hiding his face from me, and that evening, I had empathised with him so much that I had embraced him in the public!

'The lachrymal has its own story,
Sometimes intensely miserable,
And at times, terrific glory,

Weeper is the new-found love,
When lovers find solace by each other's side,
In thunderstorm, lightning, you also view a dove,

The anomalies, although are a way of bruised life,
Yet it gives a perspective of a profound sight,
Not in vain, will it drain your strength in strife,

The lachrymal has its own story,
Remember, my love, you have me around, to face good, bad, ugly and
the gory!'

7

THE STRANGER APPEARS

The train from Vasco was transitioned through many divided routes and other east heading bogies. There was no direct train from Vasco to Puri since the directions were opposite, the people and so was the culture. Obviously, my super-exciting summer internship at SNG Rudra Bank was a kind of dampener. No Jojo in it! Two months without him would be seriously a dull affair, although I was contented to be at home, but the losses were paramount. Ask someone who was indulged in love, the nascent heart-beats of love!

He had baked an eggless fruit cake for my journey, knowing that I was an authentic Odia Brahmin, with some sandwiches and cookies.

'Sweet gesture! I am so glad you cooked this for me!'

'Not really, my mom was yelling at the top of her voice because I had wasted the first cake sponge by burning it. The ancient Goan kitchen is now at a mess, a real mess. But it's worthy, Naads, looking at this brightened face of yours, all my efforts have paid off, he said smilingly but his eyes looking faint and cloudy.

I boarded the train and stood at the door, looking at his boyish lean figure, his round child-like eyes, the mole on his tiny nose, and also at the fists of his hands, which seemed to be restless that day. Hiding his emotional side, he tried to look carefree, botherless, and acted supercool. The train signalled to move; the wheels making a screeching sound, gradually drifting away from the platform where the hustle of the people kept fading, but what stood there, stilled and unmoved was a boy of eighteen, who had his saga of life, gazing at me from the bottom of his heart, silently asking me to return to his weakened self.

'Mrs Patrick, is there somebody at the door, uhmm, are you listening?'

There was no answer from Mrs Patrick. She can be a little troublesome at night! The clock said 2 am, and it was certainly a wee hour for a decent person to knock on the door! Not in my many years in this settled British land had been worrisome but today there was a terrible thought in me as if it's not right for me to answer the door. By turning on the lights, I found Mrs Patrick outside her room, in confusion, maybe the same as mine, whether or not to open the door.

'Nayan, let me have a quick check at the window,' she said and hurried to the study's window.

A dear colleague in London imposed my house, a sober purchase of my long savings. It was not an extravagant property but a quaint little hopeful house that marched onto the first rays of Sun, Moon, and the snow! It had a tiny little lawn, Mrs Patrick mowed and shaped that. The climbers gave the house an extremely warm look from the exterior. The best part about it was its size-just as much required.

Outside, the weather was full of mist, we could hardly find anyone standing there.

'Who could it be! I seldom have any visitors.'

'There's nobody, my goodness, my sleep has been disturbed, compromised,' cried Mrs Patrick.

'Calm down, please!' I said in an orderly tone.

Although sleep was her priority, she accompanied me by gazing minutely at the nearby roads, the houses opposite to ours, the fencing area, and the small steps at the facade of the condos. Nonetheless, the adventure in both of us died as the nightfall seemed a little eerie, and venturing out was certainly hushed out of the window.

'Who could it be!' my mind travelling in lightning speed to tie all the loose ends to the visit of someone stranger than strange. Sleep-deprived I was that night since many deceptiveness engulfed me, letting things unresolved. There was nobody close to me in this town, maybe a few neighbours befriended over the years, not that they would be troublesome. And there was no besotted lover to crave for, not anymore! Sighing hard, I got up from my bed that didn't tinker the bell of a fantastic life. We always miss the bygones, irrespective of how difficult or distasteful it must have been, that's us as humans, the complicated restless minds of the world.

I went back to the same window that had left me this thoughtful. I shuffled through some books, but like no other day, it didn't settle me down to read. The lone window was my sole attention that night. The sky above was extravagantly starry and luscious for a romantic encounter, especially like that of a vampire's love. While looking up and feeling empty within, I noticed some movement next to my compound's fence. Looked like a man trying to barge through…

Stunned by this, I ran towards the door all by myself!

The flight of stairs was as if a cradle of clouds. It didn't register that things could be dangerous. I opened the main gate and found that nobody except me was this jerky and excited or awake that night. I saw the tall man gazing up in a direction that led to my place, my window! The front porch lamps were switched on. I stood by the front of the door, not moving an inch towards the tall man, rather checking on his obsessive gazes. For about ten minutes, we didn't know what each other's intention was, whether or not to deliberate. While he was looking straight at me, I also realized that he was that injured man who had sought shelter at my place. It was him who I had apparently been searching for, if not frantically but subtly. It was through him that the poetess in me was brought back to life, the significant him, the stranger!

To this day, he looked better composed, calm yet unsettled in the eyes. His dark skin and hazel eyes were rather a sexy affair. His long nose with a high forehead, frown lines, and slight whiskers gave out his unspoken age of the middle life of adulthood. I brought coffee to the table where he sat like the man of this house, astounding me in all the ways.

'For you,' he spoke for the first time with his accented voice.

I saw him keeping an envelope, on top of which, a cursive 'Thank you' made an impression.

'You make good coffee, reminds me of someone,' he said with a slight smirk.

Letting no word out, I smiled slyly.

The conversation without words was odd but fascinating. By the time, he finished the coffee, we had recorded enough glimpses of each other. He left and promised to be back soon for some more cups of coffee. It gave a certain confirmation about my life suddenly filled with colourful butterflies. I didn't expect him to smile before leaving. But did it mean something?

'The bravery and helping hand speak a lot about you as a person, your heart, and your intentions as a human! Thank you for pulling me from the ditch and not letting me die.'
-Scott

8

AT THE SHORE'S END

For all the residents of Puri and all of Orissa and Bengal, Lord Jagannath was a living divinity. By the shore of the Bay of Bengal, Puri is a magical affair for all and sundry- for devotion! Hindus are permitted by all grace but people of other religious beliefs are stranded outside, in their own form of imagination, embracing the enlightenment of the Lord. It is said that the temple didn't allow Lord's utmost devotee, Salbaig or popularly known by Salabega amongst the Odias, since he was a non-Hindu, hence Salabega wrote hymns and songs devoted to the Lord. Legend says that Salabega's mother was a Brahmin widow who was abducted by Lalbaig, a Mughal *subedar*. Salabega was their only son. When Salabega was a child, suffering from illness, he was asked by his mother to enchant the Lord's name, who is also considered to be Lord Krishna. Miraculously, Salabega recovered, hence giving Puri, the devotee of a lifetime!

Unfortunately, since Salabega was of Muslim origin, his dedication was crushed by the temple guardians, he wasn't allowed inside of the temple. He was hurt but became one of the greatest devotees of the Lord. *Shreekhetra* is his abode of peace now! It is also said that once he wished to see the 'Rath Yatra' or the Chariot Festival of Puri but could not make it since he fell extremely ill. He had offered prayers to the Lord, requesting him to wait for a slight glimpse. On the return ceremony of the 'Ratha- *Nandighosh'*, the chariot didn't move until Salabega returned!

'Ma, is this story true or just myths?'

'Shhh…don't negate the stories around the Lord! Of course, it is nothing but the truth. It is about our Protector, Preserver and the Lord Himself, you dare not challenge it!'

I understood that things of religion bring the utmost emotion in people, whether for better or worse is debatable. Languishing with the non-presence of Jojo, I could hardly focus on my internship. Surely, I had realized that my dreams now were bifurcated, instead, which was alarming to a person like me. My family, who were of staunch *Brahmanical* ideologies, will crush my dream of being with Jojo, who was first a non-Odia and above all a non-Hindu! The thoughts sank my heart and my desire to be aligned with my love.

It was a Tuesday morning in May, and in the concocted weather of the Sun and the cloud, Bapa, Ma and I visited the Jagannath Temple at the break of dawn. The slight haze of the horizon, the slight hustle of the *Bada Daanda*, the sight of the over-dramatic beggars, the wrinkled old men in dhotis and *gamchas*, and the sudden appearance of white tourists, gazing at the enigmatic architecture of the great temple struck a non-neutral chord in my heart. The white devotees belonged to the 'Hare Krishna' movement by being more Hindu than me in attire and probably in belief too. Still, their dream of catching a peek of the Lord was distanced. I was of the same understanding before I had met Jojo. Things like these didn't bother me earlier, but it did now.

Cleansing my feet in the incessant small pool of water outside the entrance of the temple, didn't clear the fixes I was at. The 22 steps to reach the premises of the Lord developed a level of guilt inside me, it kept questioning me as to 'How pure a Hindu was I? How truthful was I to my belief? Was my belief challenged by the intimate relationship I shared with Jojo? Was my Hinduism now divulged? Was my Hindu blood diluted by the physical touch of a non-Hindu boy?

With my thoughts crisscrossed inside the temple, I felt a need to stop thinking about anything but Jojo. Awaiting to see the Lord, I asked my mother, was it alright of me to befriend someone of a different religion. I had never seen the Earth standstill, but that day, it did.

My mother limited her communication with me for an entire week. Now, most of her time was spent praying to God and cursing the modern outlook of youngsters. The non-followers of tradition do not have any place in our society, our community. She didn't mention my adamance to my father, who held equal beliefs and philosophy. My mother's behaviour greatly affected me because she was someone I had very high regard and deep affection for, and her infrequent cold monologues with me wrenched my heart. I thought of sharing my ongoing with Jojo, who stayed some 1600 kilometres away. The only device of communication, then, was a landline telephone. Dialling from home or my place of the internship was impossible. I chose a distant PCO telephone booth and prayed that only he and nobody else should answer my call.

'Hello,' he said in a sadder tone.

'Hey, it's me, Nayantara!'

'Naads, my love, I am drowning here with your thoughts, please come back soon and save me,' he cried.

My heart sank. I was in deep shit. I felt the need to weep, but the booth had transparent glasses, and so I composed myself.

'Not a single show was performed to its glory, not a single song I wrote. Please come back to my arms like the lights!'

'It feels so nice to hear from you, after a month and a half. How are you and your mom?'

'Mother was ill, but recovered. My voice should explain the state of my heart to you.'

'What if I decide to stay here?'

'You are a pessimist, a sadist, I knew. You want to walk past me?'

'Just engulfed by what-ifs.'

'Hmm...then I have to take a train to your land I guess, sing my heart to you again, touch you again, grab you by your waist and give you what you've been wanting now.'

'Jojo, I am in a public telephone booth!'

'My love, I am at my place of comfort. I am missing you like crazy. Don't overthink and deep fry your brain. Finish your internship, enjoy the stay at your home, and come back soon. And our love will withstand the test of all the potential differences that you are thinking about right now. Don't panic. Let the time come.'

His unruffled 'gyan' dissuaded all my negative tentacles of religious dogma, letting my heart into the bylanes of a dreamy and peaceful memory that once it was. His childlike eyes and man-like touch were the things that took my unsettled mind to him again, leaving behind my philosophical beliefs. Now, I was waiting to be held by him, although the upsetting expressions of my dear mother ruptured my heart. I wish everybody's ideologies to be in sync, which was iffy at all points of time.

'Union of two souls was a thing of ponder,

Only the touch of unified feelings was never enough,

What was abundant is always a cause of question!

Birth, Belief and astounding surroundings,

Does my love need to own them all?

Roads were uncarved, yet the journey decided,

I guess it is now not about the final destination,

Since destination will now be unnerving and too iffy,

My love, can we stand the test of these dogmas…

My heart disunites with my intelligent mind

So does my blood while pumping life to my mortal existence

Union is now a foreigner soul!'

9

WELCOME SCOTT-LAND!

For the next two weeks, the only thing my mind was unsettled about was the visit of Scott, suddenly into my safe haven. His visits were unusual just like him, mysterious and eerie to the core of unreality. He bought with him a dark side that was quite melancholic to my existence. It reminded me of my days in Goa and to some extent London. It reminded me of my desperate acts, my innate sexual lures, and my deep preserved sentiments to be with a man.

'Hi, you at work?' asked Scott on a Saturday afternoon.

'Is that you? Scott?'

'Indeed! I would love to have dinner at your place tonight. I am self-inviting me.'

He disconnected the call even before I could intervene and pause him. It was some kind of imposition, I felt, but just couldn't refrain from being outright and curt. That entire afternoon I tried analysing the reason for him to behave like my man, which he was not.

With haste, I got down to the daily farmer's market. It was kind of the outskirts of the town, hence I had to get down at the stations which come early, walk across many parks and shops to get to this place. Believe me, piling on is never a fun game. It's a mere deprecation of feelings.

Spring got me here! It was the end of March and a weekend and all I did was try to bake, toss and sauté for Mr Somebody, who was categorically a nobody in my life! Mrs Patrick had offered me help in baking the chocolate mud cake. I thought it was too heavy for supper, but she thought it was a weekend.

The dinner table was arranged and rearranged, the napkins were wedged in-between the plates and the cutlery, the sleek wine glass to one side and to the other, a regular glass for drinking water. The candles were set at the centre of the table, to which I had raised a major objection since not all motives of Mrs Patrick can be defined as ordinary!

He buzzed at the main door. Out of courtesy, I went to welcome him.

He stood there, tall and dapper, exactly at 7:00 pm, for the perfect supper at the most inappropriate of all places and in front of the most deprived woman. With his subtle grey, rather piercing eyes, he looked at me in the most suitable of ways possible. A mixture of kindness, hotness and above all attractiveness rolled in and out of his expressions.

'Invite me in,' he said.

'Is it required, haven't you already done that for yourself?'

He smiled for the first time and said, 'I thought we are friends and not just acquaintances!'

The weather had turned to be a little cooler than expected, thankfully not snowing because Rickmansworth was quite consistent to change climates. Not to be considering only the external changes, there seemed to be something very innate yet extremely vague brewing at my home too.

Mrs Patrick excused herself for the day. Although she preferred me babysitting her cutest foxhounds, Elsa and Nelsa. Elsa was a flirtatious she-dog, she cornered Scott and preferred to stay with him.

Nelsa was bored with our fine-dining and stayed aloof most of the time. He found heaven on my couch.

The entire evening passed by cuddling these two sons of a bitch, literally. I think Elsa was more enthusiastic and tried pleasing Scott with her pretty tail-wagging and drooling activities. Nelsa gave away as many deep sighs as possible.

As a matter, we seldom had time to talk about each other. It was like parents trying to strike a deal with their children. Both the dogs fell asleep. We had some time to breathe. It was a discovery to see some bright side to Scott, a side of a compassionate man, yet brooding with a lot of inner anxiety. His characteristics had so many layers, so much to unravel, so much to know about him. His past, his present, and his plans! I, for obvious reasons, didn't intrude at all. I left it to him to tell me what his persona is all about, what his existence has been through.

It was close to 11 in the night when he left for his work.

'Work!'

'Yes, Nayan!' Before this, he had never called out my name that loud. It was new to my ears, probably a Brit shortening my name and anglicizing it in the uber-most way possible. It created ripples of fantasy.

He took his coat, hat, and artfully dusted it as if he wished to stay with me for some extra hours. I couldn't stop myself but accompany him to the main door. As he bid adieu, he turned again, this time facing me. The faint light of the lamp at the threshold was trying to create some aura of romance. I could only see his tall figure and his sparkling big eyes. It gazed at me, my facial features, especially on my lips. Greatly or sadly nobody moved, as if we belonged to the static part of the Universe where everything around us had life. He exhaled, making his breath reach the core of my heart. And that's it...it was a point where our thing of friendship had begun...

We didn't kiss, and neither did we embrace to part, that night.

10

MIXED EMOTIONS

Jojo was restless. My home phone number was given to him for emergencies. After several attempts, he somehow reached me, exasperated with anxiety and feeling kind of secluded.

'Naads, it's me!'

'Hi! Were you the one calling me so impatiently, several times?'

'Sorry for that,' keeping mum for a minute.

'How are you?'

'Not great! No, you, no good music, no happy audience, and not enough money, which is alright with me. The only thing pricking me is you not being here,' he sighed.

'I will be there at the end of next month. Till then, you must be fine! Write songs of separation! Desolation opens the gate for melodious music. Take inspiration from this separation, Jojo!

'Naads, these hotel folks, where I play music, want me to take up a job in Bangalore. The money will be good as they have promised. But my studies are still on… so kind of puzzled.'

'How about your Mom?'

'She is as neutral as the lighthouse at Baga!'

'Hahaa! If you want to go for it, your studies shouldn't suffer. Ask your college administration for a correspondence course structure for you. Rather convince them.'

'That's what I have been missing…guidance! Love you. Come back soon!'

I felt better since he felt better! That was the interconnectivity that love carried, more than anything, care and compassion tops over everything else. No sooner, my contended feelings of a fruitful conversation were challenged by my mother's contemptible looks. I guess she overheard the entire conversation. Her expressions were full of hatred and disgust.

'It seems you have made all the plans of out-casting yourself,' she said and stomped her way out, slamming my bedroom's door. For sure, I was irked but later found these events as nothing but a farce. Ever since my mother's relationship with me has been a little distanced, strained.

> *'Departed souls tend to love longer,*
> *All they bear is beads of thunder,*
>
> *You not being here is nothing of glory,*
> *Alas! I am praising songs for our love story,*
>
> *My guiding star that you have become,*
> *Putting my life to a wholesome,*
>
> *Here's the happy note only in your praise,*
> *Where melody is sung to its utmost poise,*
>
> *Remembering you is now a classy affair,*
> *Since separation has interspersed a mellifluous air,*
>
> *Understanding that departed souls tend to love longer,*
> *Now there is no fear bearing the fruits of thunder!'*

A letter arrived exactly after 15 days of my conversation with Jojo! Quoting one of the most adorable songs of all times. As if the clock stopped running and the wind whistled the silkiest tunes ever. I was mesmerized and was swept off my feet. With the ripening words, Puri had become every bit of Goa.

The dreamy letter in my hand and threshold of my house was apparently not the best of places to be at. The only thing I remember to this day was a huge blow on my face, which had made me lose my balance off my feet, and all I could see was the paper being torn into pieces!

The coffee turned cold and the light outside my house shady. My impassioned and insipid mundane tale of the current years was brought to the forefront, as the darkness outside my huge window looped in. Was I turning into this gloomy, stoic writer or was I just a remorseful outcome of a love failure? Jojo's ecstatic music, his slender fingers, and his child-like eyes somehow invigorated poignancy. Even after twenty years of deprivation of his presence, my mind swung in his thoughts and craved for his music, surprisingly! I got up and tried hushing away men like Jojo, who kept wedging in between my existing life and likeness for Scott. I knew Scott was a grave, dejected man but I saw his eyes twinkle for me. Maybe I was overthinking. I saw some great depth in which he looked at me. The coffee again turned cold, this time losing its core taste. It was just bitter with no punch of its own. So, there was something about Scott that turned me on! His eyes probably…

Eyes of Wonder...

Never did I thought and maybe it was never felt that strong
The depth of your eyes that caught me to this day for long
While you spoke, your lips didn't lure
What lured is the intent of your sight!
Whether I was a fool or just a commoner in grant
How could I walk past those looks, with these many minutes gone!
Better late than never they say
And it may so be quoted,
Your eyes did wonders
Which I had missed in these many years of thunders!

Next morning, on being too perplexed by the letter dropped by Scott asking for dinner together, and besides it, a pot of jade gave me mixed thoughts yet again! Now, the convulsion that cramped my brain was...is Scott really looking for something in return? And is it primarily sexual like Ronnie, who I don't wish of mentioning...?

Mrs Patrick excused herself for a month as her daughter Nicola was seeking help in raising her one-year-old son. She was a single mother, trying to make ends meet. She was incessantly supported by Mrs Patrick. Nicola was too young to have faced widowhood. Her husband was killed in the London subway blast, which was a confirmed act of terrorism. It was so chaotic that evening while trying to find his mortal remains amongst the charred bodies of the lifeless that she vomited and was traumatized for several days. Dismayed by the entire gamut of events, she had also discovered that she had conceived the last remains of her husband. That she was made pregnant by him. It was difficult. To recoup from the death news, not finding his last mortal remains and then strangely finding his part growing inside her body. She was dejected by the truth of his non-presence but at the same time delighted by the news of her pregnancy. And who says, life can't push you for mixed emotions!

With Mrs Patrick gone to attend to her daughter, I had Elsa & Nelsa for company. Thankfully, I was quite fine with dog-sitting and it brought in me a sense of accomplishment that I too could be a mother of something. Both the foxhounds were non-disturbing elements. Rarely did they make me unleash my patience. It was comforting to have them around.

One fine afternoon, while I was down with a bad throat, I saw someone trying to enter the front gate. I was sleepy because of the antibiotics and didn't feel like investigating further. Elsa started barking aloud since she was vigilant of the screechy sound of the gate being unlatched. My drowsiness was not mitigating and hence I shushed Elsa, covering my head under the pillows, I was deep asleep.

Somewhere I felt an urge to get up since a tinkling sound made me restless. Leaving my lethargic self, I made it to the kitchen. To my horror, I discovered, the sink taps open, the used utensils undone, and the cold storage kept open! 'Thief? There never has been one.'

I found the backyard untouched, no bloodstains, no misplacement of my cutleries, no theft of my valuables. Strangely Elsa and Nelsa were at ease too.

56

11

KNOWING NICOLA

The baby kept weeping all the time these days. Also, in the passing months, as he was growing, he kept his mom on her toes for sure, and also, he made sure that there was no rest allowed to her either. Nicola from a pampered girl to a gloomy and struggling woman. She worked at an elementary school as an art teacher in the morning and also tutored a couple of neighbours' children in the evening to make ends meet.

'Not even hand to mouth, Mom!' she cried.

'Not to worry, I am here like always.'

'I am 27 and unable to take care of myself! It disgusts me,' she had few tears roll down her cheeks, and that got absorbed in her dress. 'You shouldn't have invested your time into a haggard like me.'

Mrs Patrick, all her life, toiled hard to be the provider to her only daughter. She would just go about doing anything for her, even if it wasn't necessary. She was nothing but a fairy in her life. Mrs Patrick was married to a French mountaineer who fell in love with her while she was serving him in Mount Titlis, Switzerland. She had been quite a traveller herself and explorer back in her younger days. She was assisting a professor at the University of Wales, learning about exotic gardens, where, very strangely, she was asked to take care of his travel plans to Mount Titlis. On reaching the icy white field of amusement, she almost desired to spend her entire life helping, assisting visitors of mountaineering and be less inclined to planting and decorating.

Mrs Patrick's dedication and passion extremely impressed the professor of Wales in serving the tourists and hence used his contacts to provide her a permanent job at the Mountaineering Tourists office. It was then that a French mountaineer, Gustav Emanuel, who had fallen in for her positivity and caring nature knocked at her fate. Mrs Patrick had conceived before she got married to Gustav. The adrenaline was high; it was a temperature of -10 degrees, much higher than the other days; when Gustav took Mrs Patrick into his tent quietly, switched on the French song, "Oh la'amour", and had licked her incessantly around her ears. She had given in to his raw masculinity and had grabbed his cloth ridden filament, wanting to take it inside of her. The dilation and contraction of her flesh within was uncontrollable…she sighed for his intrusion. They both were heavily clothed, which made their lovemaking process, even more delayed yet electrifying!

The next morning, as if two flushed ducks were discovered in each other's body! Bruised, bitten and invigorated! That's how Nicola was conceived. She was an outcome of Love and not the arrangement of marriage.

Nicola was blessed with one of the best features that a girl could possess. Long forehead, thick arched eyebrows with honey coloured eyes--though her nose was a little broader at the tip, but these blunt features looked even more syrupier. There was a faded mole above the depression of the upper lips; the lips were too sharp like a true European lady; the wrists were too slender when compared to her hips and stout legs. A perfect curvature depicted—Nicola, the love borne child of Mrs Patrick & Gustav.

Of time in Zurich, Mrs Patrick was addressed as Gustavia-the wife of Gustav! She would not only like it but blossom like a flower. Gustavia was an exemplary wife, the most caring and understanding that a man could dream of. She was shorter, plumper than Gustav, but with similar features that she gave her only daughter. Nicola was five feet seven inches and Gustavia was just five feet one inch! Nicola's father was five feet eleven…

Nicola's father was named Gustav by her grandmother, as she was a great fan of the romantic and revolutionary author Gustav Flaubert. Being a lady of charisma and dreams, she was very influenced by the author's portrayal of charged up, dreaming women of the 19th century so much that she had presented Mrs Patrick her favourite novel, Madame Bovary, at the time they got hitched! The nickname of Gustavia was started by none other than her.

By 35, Gustavia discovered that her husband had a pulmonary disease called edema that led to congestion in the air spaces of the lungs. The Swiss mountain doctors hence warned Gustav to shift to a lowland. A land where he mustn't trek, mustn't climb heights. Dejected with the doctor's diagnosis, Gustav with his family and no dreams had shifted to Leicester, the UK where all he could do was whine for the mountains. A year later after putting up at Leicester, when Nicola was about eleven years old, Mrs Patrick was no longer Gustavia, she was a gloomy widow.

So, all her life in Leicester, Mrs Patrick had done was work towards the comforts of Nicola, the love remnants of Gustav! Nicola was a bright student, but unlike her parents, she lacked the will to work and study. She was only a graduate of Arts with no major subjects to her credit, although she had taken up fine arts, but she was too fickle a person to stick to it for long. With great difficulty, Mrs Patrick had arranged for a job for her, that of an English grammar teacher at one of her employer's places. Nicola ended up losing the job by starting a stormy affair with the employer's younger brother, who was a law graduate from Oxford. Disgusted with Nicola's loose temperament and flirtatious character, she somehow sent her to Asmara. She was propelled to a UN mission camp as a nurse. The job was to provide help and nursing to ailing soldiers, recovering from rescue missions. It was there while nursing Daniel Wright that Nicola had fallen for his enduring nature, his sustenance in life, and his honey coloured eyes! Nicola was 24 when she walked the aisle with Emanuel at a make-shift prayer house in Asmara. Daniel was a combination of all the possibilities that a woman desire!

Their nest was quite small in Asmara but it didn't bother the moonstruck couple, their love life was quite an edgy thriller that was discussed even outside their tent. It didn't bother them since Daniel kept it quite simple, 'I am a soldier with a second life and it was only for you my love, that I breathe. Let anybody or everybody talk about our love as a gimmick, why must we care!'

Nicola, with a mind of a child, nodded to whatever her man spoke. It was guaranteed that she was in deep love with him. She would quickly finish her job in the camp and rush to her tent, where she would make her bed, prepare noodle soup, and wait for his return. Like her mother, she too played this exemplary wife in the odd hours and lust-driven lover in the right ones. They preferred sex at almost any part of the day, whenever they had time-off, or rather they found their time-offs! For an onlooker, they were two love-lost cases, always into each other, diverse in many ways yet united by love.

Dany as she would address him liked biting her full lips, her pink tongue, the fat of her breast, many a time slip his slender long fingers inside her stockings while she would gasp in surprise, play around her clitoris while she complained after the intense love-making session, grabbing her from behind, and unclothing her in a rush, as if life was running out, and it was their last time to make-out…the thrill of their love would soon end up on their couch turned bed with both moaning out of contentment, overflown fruits of passion. Those groans and yells were not shunned from the neighbouring tents, Dany's fellow soldiers and their wives. The wives would sigh in grief and happiness whereas their soldier husbands would just play ignorant!

Nicola was immersed in solitude, after the sudden killing of her beloved husband, who had given her so much to remember and so many things to miss. During nightfall, when Adrian would fall asleep to her lullaby, she would gradually, with a feather-like movement, slip out of her bed, grab her nightgown, and go out to the window to glimpse the moon. She would do that daily, without shedding a single drop of tear, without the rolling down deep story, she would just watch the moon incessantly; as if Dany looked from above. She would only imagine him and nobody else at those fugitive mythical meetings. Whether it carried any good or was insignificant, she didn't bother. For her, the hands of the clock would retreat her soul to the yesteryears with her beloved husband. Usually, this would cause fatigue of some sort, making her slump down on the floor. Realizing that the present life has Adrian, she would soon go back to him, slip inside the same way! This was cyclical and fewer times noticed by Mrs Patrick, instilling a feeling of awe and shock.

Mrs Patrick was deeply concerned about her only daughter to have cycles of eccentricity for her deceased husband. She figured out that Leicester would do no good to her daughter and grandson, except bringing back memories of Daniel, hence she accompanied her to Rickmansworth.

12

THE BITTER PAUSE

'*The whip of fresh air, the sip of citrus*
Your return is like a goldfish electrophorus!

Gazing at you from head to toe,
Has an insight to my heart to and fro!

Touch is just a mere moment,
What stays is the memories of relinquishment!

Just hold yourself steady
Let me look closer in your mind
Alas! I discover my reflection in your limitless flight!'

My hostel's room had this song slipped underneath, probably in the middle of the night! It was Jojo but him sneaking into my institution like a midnight owl was a thing of deep concern since he wasn't simply the one who would jeopardize my reputation for his wee desires. Two months at Puri had left my feelings unchanged for this guy. My only concern was our communal difference, which will not be perceived too well in my family. The trigger was already witnessed. Neither of my parents, cousins, and extended family would nod their heads for accepting this relationship. Their acceptance was of primary importance to me.

Sunday evening at Hotel Christmas Tree, the band sounded pale, without any vibrancy, since their vivacious lead singer, Jojo wasn't performing. He was attending to their sister's concern in Bangalore. The note was dated fifteen days back. Probably, he had some contact person at GIM who had probably done the sneaky act. The following days in Goa were busier in attending to new trimesters, new programs, and also new aspirations. Amongst this newness of everything, my heart wished for Jojo. His undisturbed looks at me, his slender fingers strumming incessant chords of love and longing, and yet his boyish trail wanting to achieve his goals! He was a terrific blend of blood and fire.

There were a lot of changes happening at GIM, roommates, friendship, goals, love, etc. My roomie, Reena, had incessantly fallen for a guy named Sanjeev Dogra, who belonged to Shimla and whose entire family served the army excluding him! Sanjeev was that typical mountain guy, who had a square jawline, sharp nose, deep-set eyes and a superbly fair complexion. He was some six feet tall and carried the voice of heavy bass. It seemed as if all the gravity had been pulled into his voice-box! Reena often found similarities between Sanjeev and her ex. It seemed ridiculous to me, but I kept mum. While our lady was all heart-popped up for this gravity guy, Sanjeev was reserved on most of the occasions. He didn't pay heed to what the campus people had to tease him about. He was too casual about Reena's feelings for him.

Jojo's letter of the song had nothing but the song! No contact information, no directives to get back to him. It irritated me to a great extent. So, all I did after the summer internship was wait for Jojo's arrival in Goa. The wait was full of restlessness.

'Hey, Nayantara!'

'Sanjeev, what are you doing up so late?'

'I have been waiting to ask you something,' said he, clearing his throat.

'Yes! I am listening. Go ahead.'

'How about we go out for drinks?'

'Drinks?

'Only if you want to!

'I don't drink, Sanjeev. You might want to ask Reena out?'

'I'd thought so. You would bring that up! And I have an alternative to that as well. I am expecting my cousin in a couple of days, let's all hang out at Tito's?'

'Sounds like a plan. Do you want me to ask Reena?'

'No, leave that on me. And thanks for agreeing.'

My mind didn't want to, yet it was heading in a direction that hinted to me something about Sanjeev's approach. We were always on good terms in the first few trimesters, but never too close to go out for movies or drinks. Reena would freak out! 'Huh' I sighed and buried my head into my management books.

'Saturday at 9 in the evening', Sanjeev had recalled me after the sessions. He had confirmed that Reena was a part of the evening. I was relieved, yet a little disturbed by his involvement in my interests suddenly. After a lot of debate, Reena agreed to put on the red off-shoulder dress that I had chosen for her from the Colva flea market. She was certainly conscious and uncomfortable, but I insisted her to wear nothing but that. Keeping Sanjeev's taste in mind, Reena had nodded.

Dolled up she was for sure, but she looked like a million bucks. Sanjeev would surely shift his perverse heart when he set his eyes on her. At Tito's, there was a phenomenal gathering.

'You bet it is Saturday and Goa!'

'No, I don't.'

Sanjeev was as usual a few of those smart lads who dressed just right for the occasion. His cousin was not bad either. Reena was a boozer and so was Sanjeev's cousin. I saw the attractive wind flowing in the wrong direction. Reena was only talking to the cousin and

Sanjeev was taking the utmost happiness out of it.

'Dance?' he asked me. I was nervous, about to bite my nails when the sudden announcement at the bar saved my plight. Some bands were performing, and they were from the rock capital, Bangalore.

'Hey, guys! Welcome to our band's first performance in Goa!'

The crowd cheered the band called Escapists. The name was too absurd for a music band but of-course they would have their own sweet justification for it.

'Ladies, we have Jonathon Rodrigues as lead guitarist and vocalist along with Tulip Shetty.' The audience in us hooted and cheered as Tulip was a ravishing beauty. Jonathon's entry was dramatic with disco lights flickering in and out. We could hardly see him. Sanjeev pulled me out of the entire gamut of events. I was furious, and he was romantic. He held my hands in a fashion that only lovers hold. He was about to speak when I forcibly pushed him aside and made my way inside the bar. It was impolite of me, agreed but not improper of me.

'Jojo! You in Goa!' I cried in the high amplitude surrounding.

'Jojo is Jonathon Rodrigues! Did you know? Crazy stuff this is!' Reena came looking for me almost drunk.

'Let's just leave, Reena! The night is turning out to be more horrible than a nightmare.'

And we left.

There was a card from Jojo stating that he had to move to Margao for yet another performance of his. This pricked me even more so much that I buried the card inside one of my old textbooks.

'Something has changed, isn't it?'

'He's just keeping busy. Trying to do well in life!'

'No! Jojo has changed for sure and not for good!

Reena, like any other caring friend, tried all gimmicks to lighten up my mood, but a cheated heart listened to nothing. Jojo's terrible act of discretion had left me meddlesome. It was difficult to answer the 'yes or why' of it. It was simple. Our love story was simple. What got into it!

Sanjeev kept trying his luck with me, but I was too hurt and not ready for another nonsense of romantic occurrence. I decided to confront Jojo whenever it would be. Sometimes, it's so eerie to understand that people who push you into relationships are the ones to flee first, with no reasoning or compassion. I was hurt deeply. Every passing hour of the day, no matter how much I tried, was rather difficult to ignore the memories that were so fresh. From fresh to stale; I was a distorted mind. My mind wandered in all thoughts of misinterpretations, ridiculous thoughts, and restlessness. And there was no help. Since when did I turn from an ego-laden strong female to a love-struck sickening soul, when? I'd questioned myself often to me. But I understood it sooner that only I could fix this part, I could only mend this fissured heart, this deep cut!

I didn't curse Jojo because I allowed everything that happened. I didn't stop things. We always have a choice to stop events or people. I got it clear. By the time I was recovering, my fourth trimester had suffered pretty badly. From a six-point five grader to a four-point grader, the travel backward in studies was surely a failure shaking hands with me but was a curve of learning too! It made me introspect and analyse that the big word "love" was actually not for odds like me!

I completely owed the blame on me and nobody else since I was primarily involved with a local fellow, younger than me! Probably it was a complete mismatch and contempt to my outlook. Sometimes, parents don't shout in vain!

There was no news from Jojo henceforth, and back then we were in an age where social media didn't take the youth by a storm! I detested my relationship with Jojo, although wasn't quite successful in keeping him out of my mind. Somebody directed me to yoga!

The final trimester was not a speedy recovery in GPAs. I could pull off only a five-point-eight, but there was some improvement than before. The campuses were on. The mesmerising weather looked tensed, filled with anguish, anxiety, and uncertainties of each other's future.

13

Scott & Me- At Odd's End

'Define attraction?' I asked Scott.

'Charm.'

'Define?'

'Adjust with a word of interpretation.'

Scott with his deep-set blue eyes looked at me straight and tried to study my expression of angst. He placed his palms over mine softly and said, 'Focus on the game of Scrabble and not on me. Other than minimalism, I can hardly give you anything. I don't believe in love since I haven't fallen in love for a long time now. Don't expect a lot out of me since it'll disappoint you often,' said he and looked down.

I appreciated his blunt honesty but at times I do not require such reasoning and openness. He might have probably misread my interest in him. Must have tagged me the love-struck emotion-laden woman! Yes, usually men stereotyped me as the lonely lady desperately waiting to be in love! Some years back, it was a dangerous zone to be at since I tried explaining but today, I was too full to react. Who would explain to these self-indulgent men that being single and being lonely are two different facets of life? I was single by my choice and not out of compulsion.

'Scott, other than a glass of wine, I have no answers to your apathy!'

We clicked the glass of rose wine, which was quite feisty in cooling my senses. I won the game! Scott was intelligent but too restless and not that great with spellings. So, as per the challenge, a person winning the game of scrabble was given the power to ask anything that they want.

'I want to visit the place you stay,' I demanded Scott.

'Why not!' he said and nodded the head with the same ease at which his usual conversations were.

Most weekends, Scott was traced at my place. Sometimes cuddling the hounds and helping me in cooking and finishing house chores as Mrs Patrick was out with Nicola. Elsa and Nelsa were my responsibilities now, suddenly, I was a parent of two hounds!

Once in a shower, the shower stopped pouring water and Scott shouted for help. The door was unlocked and probably the shower outlets blocked. I rushed for his help, without realizing that he was almost naked. It was an absurd encounter since I never witnessed his manhood! He, gasping after the shout out, frantically looked for something to cover his privacy. He failed miserably. I giggled at this hugely built man behaving like an unprotected adolescent. That incident left both of us a little uncomfortable to look at each other.

Scott left two days later for his work, which was still a mystery to me! His job was unknown, and he had always left in the wee hours, without passing on too much information. The only thing I have heard him saying is, 'it's too risky, but he enjoys the thrill!' My mind sometimes infer that he must be a gangster or a smuggler, because both involve risk and pump up thrill.

I didn't call or message Scott for about a week from that day because of the dilemma I was having about his role in my life. Suddenly, it felt as if I am staying with a man with no relationship quotient, any emotional bond being spoken out. He seemed to be quite comfortable as he described himself as a man with no strings attached, pragmatic to the core and yet carrying a few threads of compassion. Unlike women, he didn't carry any baggage of emotion. Relationships were a matter of neutrality for him; a mere source of attaining his manly needs.

A week without communication, although was difficult to maintain but not unattainable. I stayed within myself with Elsa and Nelsa. Both of them upgraded my living status from a single woman to a pet parent. It was relieving to be living with pets, who didn't conveniently mix practicality when it was time to show emotion! Men of today are more about fulfilling their arms of requirement than love somebody unremittingly with no preoccupancy!

That weekend was loads of household work since I'd planned to visit India to meet my parents. It had been long since I had visited them, almost two years! They were upset for a lot of reasons: first, since I was single at 39, didn't plan to maintain my legacy through a child, and second, I was overtly independent and living by myself in a foreign land. Neither we shared letters of sorrow nor did we talk over the phone for two years; the only contact person was my age-old cook, who kept calling at all possible Odia occasions to remind me of my roots.

I shopped for a 18 karat diamond pendant with a rose gold chain for my mother, although I knew that she was a 22 karat desi gold person. For my father, I selected a cot wool jacket with a few statement t-shirts, a few chocolates, perfumes and fine woollen sweaters for a few extended relatives. The plan was for two months. I planned to stay in Puri for a month, visit Mumbai for 2 weeks, Bangalore for a few days and then live in Pondicherry for a week, back to Puri and then fly off from Mumbai. Goa was out of my schedule…

The tickets were done. I was waiting for Mrs Patrick to take over the responsibilities of her hounds first and then my house. I didn't inform Scott, since his unemotional side had caught me up! I was flying by the month end, on the 29th of October to Delhi. There were over ten days to my India trip when on that fateful night Scott showed up with no significant information. I was furious, and he seemed bruised, demanding! I figured out that he only showed up when he needed some kind of nursing and attendance from me. I found this quite opportunistic and delightfully wrong!

But the need of this hour was to assist him since he was weak. There was nobody to help me on this. It flustered me for sure, but I did the aid that was required of me as a human being. Elsa and Nelsa were put to their respective beds. The last time I'd a check on Scott, he was in my study, putting his eyes to sleep.

I was in sleep when I felt some wetness around my neck! I was super shocked and immediately got up from my sleep. I looked around and didn't find anybody, which was yet another fearful factor. Have I been wet dreaming all this while! Taking a glass of water, I strolled in the living area where the hounds were deep asleep, I went to the study and didn't find Scott. Well, it didn't perturb me as he might have been in the restroom or something. I looked outside the window from the study. The sky was full of bright colours and sparkling stars. It was not at all those scary nights. Relaxed, I headed to my room.

The hands felt locked, and the mouth was sealed. I was claustrophobic! Whether dreaming or reality, it was a difficulty this time. It was a feeling of anxiety, as if a heavy body was pressing hard against mine, entrapping my free-will from all sides. I opened my eyes and saw a face in real life. His body was as warm as hell. He was half unclothed. And I was completely losing my senses in this act of physicality. The comforter was losing its shed, its end tightened by some force heavier than me. I was holding tight to it, thinking it to be my guarding soul. But alas, the soul was ripped apart. The head was too obstinate in its movement, shuddering my clit, not allowing me a second to think. I was trying to hide my orgasm, which was reaching its peak when his body brushed roughly on mine. The lamp's dim light was reflecting on the passionate bodily action that was accelerated. My nightgown was pulled off me, leaving me bared, as if after this long I was baring my soul to somebody unknown, some devil who was trying to instigate my inert desires!

The inner garments were torn off me! His body was now hard and looking to rest in my cave but before that he groaned heavily, astonishing me with his intense manly needs. My legs were tired underneath his heavy built, now his muscular wrists tried separating its union! He pulled my legs apart, quivering my sex to contain his now…there was a sudden gush of pelvic rhythm, tightening my vaginal walls and letting me reach my first orgasm after ages! Surprisingly looking for his love all over me! His tongues brought in joys from all the planets of desire! I finally gave in! My frivolous wants to take control of my conscientious mind. The dopamine speeding up to my brains; the adrenaline in its full heat and our bodies cuckolded into some boastful union.

Scott woke me up the next morning, bringing me a surprise bed tea. I had lost all rationale last night, my body still failing to wake up to the Sun and face the world of Scott everywhere! Yes, I was embarrassed about last night…

'You fine?' enquired Scott looking at my facial disgust

'Well I am not, and I cannot hide it under the sheets!'

'Last night, your actions narrated a different story, my darling!'

'It was, with all probable directions, a mere need of two bodies,' I was curt. 'Phew…have tea and cool down your senses, it's wrecked now,' Scott left the tea at my side and left.

There was absolutely no guilt and feeling of remorse after the stroke of conversation with him. I'd rather felt light-hearted after I conveyed that it was a requirement and nothing else. Suddenly, I felt empowered, winning the game and tricking the trickster! I didn't see Scott around Rickmansworth for the next couple of days. My emotional quotient didn't miss him either. In the meantime, Mrs Patrick showed up with Nicola and her son, Adrian, giving me some surprise-shock element.

Nicola was an unprecedented woman of charm! She had honey coloured eyes; the cutest nose possible but a forehead of a worried woman. Unmatched was her looks with her physiognomic expressions.

I was carried away by this young splendour and felt remorseful that the circumstance of terrorism widowed her. It was consciously decided to put her into the job-- Nicola as my personal assistant and offer her a reasonably decent pay to survive! Mrs Patrick was the most relieved mother in the soil of Rickmansworth. She felt not only great but indebted to me. Her protectiveness and regards grew deeper.

'My Gallery of Happiness

My gallery of happiness should never be sketched,
As it would leave indelible marks even in the lowest of trench

The galleria that we all have been seeking
Isn't it full of myth, pain and inkling?

Happiness is such profound entity
…craving for it would result in higher depravity

Hence, let's not crave and chase the mystical chastity
As it can be discovered within minds full of intensity'

Nicola in the couple of days helped me arrange my unorganized shelves, clothes, old magazines, discarding redundant stuff, etc. and packing my luggage for India, preparing my itinerary, book my hotels, travels, almost every goddamn thing! Let me confess that she was quite a smart cat at these bookings! No sooner, the entry of Nicola in my life brought in a lot of freshness, fragrance and organization. Her son was nothing but an angel, and after my work every evening, I spent quality time with the hounds and the baby! Life seemed enriching with home away from home and with no Scott in it!

It was already a Saturday and by Monday early morning I was scheduled flying to New Delhi, my much-awaited trip after two years! I was thrilled, anxious and also nervous, going through a lot of jammed up emotions. Last time when I was at Puri, my parents tried to hitch me up with a man who was not only ten years elder to me but was a widower with two kids! I hated that idea of getting settled with a man who wanted a mother for his children and not a wife! My parents apparently have a belief system that once girls are above thirty, their sale-ability in terms of marriage or finding the so-called husband diminishes by fifty percent; more than 35, eighty percent, hence the window of single men who are smart and intelligent is just taken by some other younger female! Hence, the options remain in adaptation to a role of a 'foster-mother' and not just a 'wife' or 'lover'! In reality, it was stranger than it sounds!

The last trip was fruitless since my own parents thought of me as a redundant old piece of furniture, which needed tarnishing by another ruined one! Just because I was 37 back then, single, yet quite content and prosperous, independent, factors of diligence were bereft from me; for the mere fact that I was unmarried! When one's family is incapable of understanding you, driving back home didn't make any point at all!

The night of 27th October brought in Scott yet again, not so surprisingly though. I wasn't waiting to bid him a 'goodbye', but they say that when you don't expect it to rain, all you get is a hailstorm!

'You don't seem joyous.'

'Actually, you read me quite correctly this time.'

'We were so good together until the night happened. Was it a burdensome experience for you?'

'It was fruitless…void actually since we made love without even falling in it! Quite absurd, isn't it? Men like you don't want love, which is a concentrated pulp of emotion, but the act of making it which you often refer to as a non-serious, easy to get-rid-of fuck!'

Scott breathed deeply, pursing his lips, at times biting it, clarifying that my conversations were piercing and bewildering. I watched his eyes rolling, his sighs turning deeper, his gestures falling completely out of sync with his 'trying to look unaffected' by emotions. At the core of my heart, I turned a little of a sadist, enjoying his looks of despair. There was complete silence in the study that we sat in. The cold air was lingering, dashing between two personalities of varied needs.

'Would you mind?' I stood up and excused myself out of the room.

'Naads!' he called me! It jittered me. Reminded me of Jojo, taking me many years back yet again.

More surprised than shocked as I was about to turn my back, as if a heavily laden ship dashed at my waistline. He held me at the small of my back and giving no thoughts to the surroundings began kissing me vehemently. The brain was zapped, the neuro-transmitters went hither and thither, the hormones took over and unwillingly, I succumbed to the fearsome desires. His hands went all over me, as if he was feeling me up for that one last time, as if life was supposedly ending on this earth, as if an apocalypse was engulfing humanity.

It was odd since he was almost six inches taller than me. Making out seemed jeopardized! It was difficult to handle a giant force of such dominance. He put all his energy on my petite body, gently pushed me onto the rug that was unrolled next to the foyer where a tiny miniature of Parisian doll was placed with a picture of my family. I didn't resist since the entire set of occurrences was too steamy and the night seemed warm, yet moony. The moonlight shone on his dusky-golden muscular body; he was naked, and all I did was look at his beautiful well-ribbed chest, abs descending to his well-exposed manhood! He was so charming in all the worldly and poetic way possible. His eyes placed on my lips, his fingers caressing my chest in all upswing movement possible. He rolled me down, his mouth on my breast, biting it hard, his hands reaching out for my pyjamas, untying the strings and pulling it off my safe haven. Choked me and was trying hard to give him a good fight, but my hands were stretched to the other end of my head. I gasped, running out of air, his mouth full of my breast, as if he was the sole possessor of it. There was a sudden traction in my cunt when his fingers were lingering over it and in a gush of time, he fingered me, trying to reach to the zenith of my spot! I came in a rush and moaned out of exasperation. Within a few seconds, I was on top of him, taking charge of the action, letting out my timid self, evaporate in the foreplay of dominance! I reached for his filament and began drawing it deep inside of me. He was weak and cried for more! His hands trying to press my chest hard, and I religiously punishing him with my bites and slurps. It was a sexual combat of sorts, where both forces took the peace out of each other.

In a sudden move, he sat up and pulled me on top of him. He entered me in all his godly forces and then began the swift movement of pelvic eroticism!

14

RODRIGUES IN THE MEMORY LANE

'The night fell quiet and joyful, isn't it, Nayantara?'

I looked with my eyes wide open since I got the knack that Nicola saw us entangled the previous night, and why wouldn't she…we were into each other in the living room, which has no door, no shades, no partitions, no curtains retaining our cloistered moments to us!

I smirked with the only guilt of a young-widow girl watching me in the submerged valley of temptations.

'I am sorry if you took offence! In actuality, I didn't mean any. Me and Daniel used to do it all l the time!' she said with a giggle.

'Daniel and you were in love, Nicole, I am not in love with Scott!'

'Who knows what defines that thing with wings! All of us have defined Love as per our own understanding and parameters, as per our experiences, good ones and sometimes wrecked ones too.'

To think of it, she made so much sense. We have all moulded and bent love in our own ways. Love is an intangible piece of feeling, which gains or doesn't gain a shape or is shapeless, sometimes a fit and at others a misfit! Hence, love can be interpreted in all directions possible!

'You talk poetry?'

'Not really into it though.'

'Would you arrange another task for me while I am gone?'

'Sure. Ask.'

'You'll find a few pieces of papers loosely tied in the drawer's chest next to the foyer in the study, some with scribbles, quite old and very few new…would you arrange them properly as per topics/dates/mood or typewrite them if you know someone?'

'Oh, wonderful to know that you are a writer too!'

'Not a serious one for sure. Extreme junk I write. Just do something to arrange it, please. It's kind of dear to me.'

'Please be assured that I'll guard it with my life, Madame!'

'No Madame, please! And thank you!'

Leaving for the London Heathrow airport almost at midnight, left me convulsed in the words of Nicole. Was there any dimension of Love that I have missed? Marriage is a social stamp and not an outcome of love, it's an outcome of everything but love!

The flight to New Delhi was full of Sardars and Sardarnis, with their big and small belongings tugged into itsy-bitsy cabin bags. Thankfully, the web check-in helped me with an aisle seat and an Indian old lady as my co-passenger. No sooner, I dozed off with Nicola's perception about love…

Campus placements were in full swing, and I was the second person to get through in the initial days of my placements. Sanjeev and I got through the same financial services as Management Trainees. Few were envious, and some very indulged in seeking their goals. As if life's motive was reaching at a job, the ultimate horizon!

My story with Jojo was unfinished, stuck in that café bar where neither we could look at each other nor we could exchange a few words of love and despair. At that point, I was furious but after some-time, I started searching for the reason for his anomalous behaviour, although

I must agree that it's never a great feeling to be blatantly ignored by a loved one! It's undergoing chains of emotions where there's no settled place to resolve!

A couple of months later, Sanjeev had again shown some courteous interest in me and this time I pondered, why not! Disinterested for sure, but keeping every human emotion aside, I let Sanjeev march ahead in impressing me. Thankfully, the place he chose for our meeting was not Tito's! It was one of the most reclusive abodes, almost touching the outskirts of Margao. It was a resort. Goa beholds many of it.

It was a sunny morning, although slightly breezy, there were few poolside musicians playing Beethoven symphony no. 5, one of his magical creations ever! Jojo had told me while playing it on the Cello. I was musically inclined because he was too drawn towards it. It was his passion. While I imagined him in my lost romance, Sanjeev stepped into my thoughts with a greeting and a bouquet.

'Hey, thanks! It's not my birthday today!'

'I know Nayantara.'

'For what is the bouquet, then? Huh?'

He pulled his chair closer and fiddled with his wrist band. He seemed nervous.

'Nayan,' his voice deepened and placing his hands on mine, he said, 'Marry me!'

Audacious he was, but it was a shocking revelation that he placed his blissful interests in me and how! Suddenly, by proposing to me to marry him. Of all people him! I truly miscalculated everything. Reena would be devastated, and I was cursing myself to go out with him.

Rushing out of that place would have been inappropriate and discourteous, hence I let Sanjeev do all the talking. He narrated about his past girlfriends in school and how he was seriously involved with somebody in his 12th, so much that they had got hitched after getting their first job, by the age of 24! Without disclosing her name, he talked non-stop that evening. His girlfriend was short and petite, had light brown hair, skin tone as light as a white rose, supple fingers, broad forehead, arched eyebrows, tiny eyes, round lips with a black mole at the edge of the lips. How she was a calm, relaxed, and 'let's never fight' person. Within three years of their relationship, how they had hardly fought once and after realizing the hurt, held each other tightly with tears rolling down, promising each other not to fight ever again!

Sanjeev paused. His face was turning pink. He looked to his left at the bar counter and gestured to the server to get two lemon iced tea, mostly composing himself. Clearing the lump in his throat, he regained his senses and said that by the time Sanjeev got through GIM, his girlfriend was sent off to Australia to study further. It was a trick to get her married to a guy of her parent's choice. She couldn't stand against her parent's wishes and had accepted the imposed fate.

I patted his shoulder, 'Courage my friend!' and smiled.

'With you, all is possible,' he added, holding my hands. 'Take your time in thinking through it.'

'What?'

'My marriage proposal. We can spend more time together. You can ask me anything.'

I felt uncomfortable when he talked about marriage. It was a 'No' I knew but didn't want to burst his bubble of hope suddenly.

'Have you told this to Reena?' I asked since I was aware of her feelings for him.

'Yes!'

'Huh? You told her you want to marry me? Isn't that insane?'

'Not at all. It is simple. Insanity would have been to hide my feelings.'

'Whatever! You are insensitive!'

'Today's insensitivity is tomorrow's awareness.'

He said and gave me a quick smile as if I had already accepted his proposal. His tall figure and handsome looks pricked me, irritated me. However, he was relaxed, very much himself, and sipped the lemon iced tea to his glory.

Without informing Sanjeev, I took up the job at Bangalore, which didn't make me guilt-stricken at all, I was not at all in love with him and neither was I solely or partially accountable for it. I couldn't have been spiteful for my friend Reena, who had instilled deep emotions for Sanjeev! How can men not understand that living beings run by emotions and alterations of such nature is vehemently disturbing to the heart; that women are also to be considered as living beings!

The weather of Bangalore differed from Goa! Cooler, non-humid, and pleasant, if I could remember it! The pub culture was gradually taking its pace and getting into the bloodstream of the young, however, the local rituals and tradition was also too foundational in the veins of the city. My office was in a place called Whitefield; this place as far as your eyes could go had nothing but a few buildings being sluggishly constructed. The residential area was, however, quite famous since it was established in the 1800s by Anglos. It had a quite posh and settled vibe to offer. I rented an apartment with a few other female colleagues of mine. It was a decently structured two-room flat, shared by three people. The only pocket crunching feeling was paying three months' rent in advance!

The apartment where I was resting started quivering! It was an odd emotion. I couldn't control it. A voice was trying to calm me down. I opened my eyes and realized that I had fallen asleep and the flight was experiencing turbulence. The seat belt signs were on and everybody was a little shaky; probably the plane was cutting through a huge chunk of cloud! I was patient, not anxious at all! Most of the people seemed disturbed! Somehow, I knew this was not my end, hence I was stable enough to run through it and again went back to sleep.

Attending one of these pubs in Bangalore on a Saturday evening brought the Instrumentalist like the first gush of rain in the monsoons! He had lost weight! My heart ceased to function. I had frozen that night, incidentally meeting him at one pub where there was laughter, energy, lights, music but also a broken heart. He played the Cello exceptionally well. He could play any string instruments with the same delight. Just that his face seemed paler than before, absolutely no vibrancy. Was he still stuck with me? I had so many questions that night, and my answer was right in that place.

'Jonathon, how have you been?' I called him.

He turned his gaze and was standstill with his Cello. There was absolute quietness in our communication, only the face unfolded the lost saga. It was melodramatic for sure. My friends interrupted in-between.

That night he didn't let me revisit my glorious days of love, rather he made sure his love was rekindled through his next piece of gig. He played vehemently. The crowd was stunned and so were his bandmates. Whether it was us or just fate! Everything was magical again!

That extravagant night, he had dared to ask me to move in with him. I denied. He complained. I still denied.

Don't call me Jonathon. It feels as if I have been distant to you!'

'Well, you were away. Pay the price.'

'Without you Naads, a year is the throttling price I've paid.' A tear of reunion rolled down on his chiselled cheeks. His small sharp nose breathing out deeply. His slender long fingers reaching out for mine.

'I am pursuing a degree in music and arts at Christ College.'

'Really! I am so glad to hear that Jonathon!'

'Call me what you were calling me!'

'Bring me back a year then...'

After the gig, he wanted me to accompany him to his place. He said that he wanted to catch up. I agreed without acting difficult. We took an autorickshaw to his place. It was not an apartment; it was an old Portuguese settlement with angelical windows. I was so surprised to find a Goan house in the outskirts of southern soil.

'Beautiful house, Jonathon!'

'It's owned by an old Anglo couple. The children stay abroad. The lady is a little stricter than the old guy. I have an entire room with a wishful corridor to myself at a very reasonable price,' he blushed and looked straight into my eyes. I knew that was an invitation of all kinds. He took his hands and placed it on his chest, trying to feel the thumping of his heart. We were standing at the gate, with no passer-by around. We lost track of time and he forwarded his steps to kiss me on the forehead. I let my chin up with all the blissful feelings getting exchanged under the moon of this night. We embraced after a full revolutionary year. He held my hand tightly and slowly sneaked into the house and eventually his room. I could expect the series of events that were about to follow but this time I didn't hold myself back.

The flight landed with a slight jerk at New Delhi's T3 terminal. The much talked about rather. The sudden jolt woke me up from the warmth that we had shared that lustrous night. It was the first time we had felt each other this enormously, this deep. Pre-landing in my home country made me delve into the memories of Jonathon Rodrigues, who was now a memory, a past. Time makes us delve into oddities of life, sometimes these oddities are infinite, till we live or till the last breath of our lives.

Human beings- the most intelligent of all living beings and yet the oddest and complex lot. Who made us complex, we ourselves! But in my complexities, Jonathon Rodrigues stands like a tall statute of bliss. His belief in me that even I could fall in love with someone so distant from every aspect of my life, was marvellous!

I giggled while picking up my luggage from the conveyor belt.

'Miss, you have an adorable smile!' said a voice as close as the air.

While turning to the unfamiliar voice, I found an unfamiliar, grey-black French bearded man, eyes too kind yet twinkling with flirtatiousness, tall nose with a black mole at the right edge of the nostril, skin milky white when compared to the average Indian brown, eyebrows thick but well curved, allowing a shape to the fish shaped eyes. His smile was dimpled, stressing his overlapping teeth, which too was a top-up in his adorable looks! He had developed crow-feet, narrating his experience in this world. What I could sum up from this gentleman was that he was an extremely smart looking chap.

'You could've thought of a better line than this cheesier one.'

'Haha…Miss, I'm old school, trying to keep up with the new dating liners though!'

'We just met! And you are referring to dating as a basis? Huh?'

'It was just a reference,' he smirked.

'You seem too fast, Mister!'

'Not really Miss! There's something about you that's very intriguing! I am trying to figure that out!'

'You are a smooth talker, aren't you?'

'If you say so…'

15

LIVING A CUP OF TEA

Only he talked! About his profession from a housekeeper to a Michelin Star Chef. From a lower middle-class Ludhiana guy to an Elite Mumbai Bandra resident! From miserably failing his 10th grade to topping at his hotel management institute in Kolkata. From an introvert unsocial to an outgoing expert; smiling and cracking jokes, complimenting ladies of grace, easily befriending gay men, stomping around with the younger lot to badly wanting to own a pet home. Only he talked! On the flight from New Delhi to Mumbai.

'You are a great listener!'

'Thanks,' I smirked since he was conscious that he didn't let me speak.

'So, when do we meet for tea?'

'Sorry!'

'You don't have to be sorry. I drink tea, all kinds!'

I didn't smile this time, but he insisted on visiting his restaurant in Colaba.

'A shanty little place,' he laughed and handed me his visiting card that had all his updated contact details.

'Just to inform you, I'll be going to Singapore the day after for a small three-day tour, work you see! You take your time and meet me after Thursday, okay Miss…huh?'

'I'll think about this,' I said shaking his hands.

'Life is too short for this worthless thinking. Engage your mind in thinking through important stuff, not stints like these! See ya, Miss!'

'See you!'

Whoa! He was some gush of energy and extravagance yet carried a mild and softened heart. Seemed to be honest, uninhibited about life and meeting new people, dropping by a smile since he said it hardly costs a cent. He was a bundle of light that kept brighter as the minute passed. But I was still undecided about meeting him. I didn't want to meet yet another good-looking man for a teaser release in my life.

Thankfully Nicola had made my hotel reservations at a great place in Colaba, coincidentally! Although the sudden change of climate change from winters to tropics exaggerated my health, failing me and slushing me to bed for three days! There were multiple calls from Puri since my plan was to take a flight within two days to Bhubaneswar for Puri. My parents called many relatives who resided in Mumbai to attend to me while I was sick. The hotel's concierge was cooperative enough to allow each one of them with minimal intervention. Thankfully, the appointed doctor at the hotel was the one who helped me recover faster and not just robbing yet another NRI guest! My relatives bought all sorts of boiled food, from *dalema* to *santula* to half cooked rotis! Amid irritation, I still found peace and home.

Rizvi N. Khaitan's visiting card seems to be an example of an emerging and globalized India! It read Head Chef with an animated chef hat and the contact details below. The card was extremely creative and not one of my bland office-goer ones! It was bright, and I could relate it to his personality, which was shiny too! However, I didn't call him since the idea seemed too rushed and childish. On getting well, I visited my friend Reena, who was now engaged to be married to his long-dating boyfriend.

Reena belonged to the eternally wealthy side of the Indian population and the corporate bug had made her a lot more extravagant than she was back in Goa. Thanks to my tropical illness, I'd missed most of her elaborated wedding festivals and could only arrive at the engagement ceremony. She was a north Indian getting married to yet another one of the same terrains. The hotel, God knows why, provided me an overstated vehicle! I was the only one travelling! I guess that's what these people do to the guests, pamper and spoil them but it's just not the real India. Real India is a struggle, to make ends meet and one can notice that in the roads and by-lanes of these cities. It is such a contradiction, inside the hotel and out on the roads! All my eyes could perceive out of Mumbai was people, in every millimetre of my retina, people were bustling with thrills of their lives, so many thrills rather!

Humid yet a little pleasant was the weather outside, thankfully Reena didn't get married during the rains…for sure, I wouldn't have been attending then. I wore a sari after a long time! The foreign land had sucked out the desi in me, at least in my external appearance, however internally I am always a seeker, sometimes a troubled one.

When old pals meet in a city of dreams, there's the beating of drums, dancing of the trees, and rhythmic sway of the breeze! Yeah! It was ditto! A poetical meeting with Reena! She'd put on some weight at her girth, could be termed as a chubby woman of 40! However, she'd hardly developed crow's feet, wrinkles or pale skin! She was very effervescent. She looked absolutely gorgeous, her skin glowing with a natural blush, the mauve lehenga --a Bollywood killer! Graceful and sexy was the entire aura of Reena! She was short, but she'd always been a pretty tomboy at GIM but look at her now, she was nothing but a ravishing lady!

We embraced each other! I knew that the lehenga was intricately designed and didn't want the sequin work to be affected by this. She was least careful, the same natured tomboy, and asked me not to worry about these silly attires! I had never met Reena's long-time beau in person although we'd exchanged a few pleasantries online and he is the perfect gentleman for her. Much better than Sanjeev.

'I've invited him too!'

'What on earth made you do that? Huh?'

'You! Nayantara, this invite is for your company. He shared his feelings about you many years back, when we graduated, and you moved to Bangalore. He was deeply mesmerised by you then and probably now too!'

'Hey, girl! Just because you are getting hitched, doesn't mean I'll want to be too! Please stop being a parent! Not fair!'

'Ufff! The same headstrong you.'

I would never try to get you hitched, but you knew this guy who was interested and seems he's still…give him a chance, what's the bloody harm?'

'I am in India to meet my folks, see you get married, and that's all! There's no relationship agenda with me!'

'Nayan, think about it. He's a great guy who's still counting his stars to be with you.'

'Are you serious, Reena! It sounds so teenaged! This wait, this love-prone bedazzled guy, the yesteryears, the heartful people… everything is just so rosy, but my life hasn't been rosy and over time I have accepted it that way. Now almost nearing 40, accepting yet another person in my life is just tough. And marriage is just not me! No man can adjust with me and vice versa!'

'You should allow people if things didn't work, not necessarily, it's going to be the same. We don't lead recurring lives! We learn! And hence must move on!'

Out of the blue horizon, where the earth meets the sky, Reena tried her best in convincing me that there's no harm to space by allowing another human. I was certainly not keen on Sanjeev. I'd never been, and I'll never be, but her words made sense to me! A loner can share too! Scott shared my space at my apartment with no sort of love commitment, with no verbal agreement to live together. But we did in a sort of way, we were living together.

'Miss, you owe me a meeting over a cup of tea?'

I turned and guess what I found… the smart chef yet again, at Reena's wedding!

'Stop following me, Mister Rizvi,' I said with a smirk.

'Thank God! At Least you smirked! Good progress,' he said it with a sly smile and slightly giving out that killer dimple on his face. 'And you remember my name!'

'It's not a big deal for me to remember names.'

'For me it is! So, why are you following me in Mumbai? You could have simply called me up?' He said and still had that lingering grin on his face.

'Stop playing smart.'

I am always you see!

'Reena is a friend of mine. How about you?'

'Reena's your friend! Good to know about that establishment. Though, I have a very close connection with her family.'

'Please elaborate.'

'You are getting entwined in my conversations, aren't you?'

'Forget it! I think you are needed in the kitchen.'

'Oh! Not to worry about my kitchen since I have sous chefs looking after the occasion's delicacies today! It's oriental and Indian fusion. But hold on, I have an interesting lady coming my way! Catch you later, Miss…'

Rizvi was an intelligent, effervescent, and restless man. I think he ran by electricity! He was too energetic to be true. Was he under the influence of marijuana? Did he have a jumpstart before he started for work, I hardly know, but he was this ball of fire that couldn't be avoided. I saw him from a distance, trying his best foot forward to win the beautiful lady in the tangerine dress. Within a span of 30 minutes, he walked past her! I gave him a look of doubt to which he just twitched his eyebrows and gestured not to be interested in her anymore!

It was funny to see a man giving up after 30 minutes of trying to seek a woman. In that way, Scott was putting up with my mindlessness for quite some-time now. But things with Scott don't hold any good since he's an uncertain, secretive man. He hardly shares his life. Amidst these futile inferences about men, I moved to a secluded corner of the lawn where a table was neatly decorated with no accessories to show off. I sat there quietly and looked from a distance at the whole pre-wedding scenario.

Reena's auspicious future life was planned here with such pomp and show. It was an extravagant celebration for just two people to unite and say, 'I do.' What was the need of such pompous when only a handful will be later concerned for their well-being? Why spend a million on something that was so basic in our life! The lawn was around four thousand square feet with beautiful plants and gardenia. The Mumbai wedding planner did their best to scale it up to the showbiz decoration, with everything contemporary and chic! The flowing drapes, the shimmering toned downlights, and the ever-chirpy wealthy people added to the glam of the occasion but the need for it was still questionable and fantastical.

Living my life to the fullest with Jonathon in the ancient Portuguese style house was like walking amid sparkling clouds. We lived together for almost a year in the most secretive way possible. It was not possible for Jonathon to stay at my place since it had other female house members in it. Hence, I played a bad roommate and a caring girlfriend. I cooked at my rented apartment and fed it to him. The initial episodes of cooking were as hell as the kitchen mess itself. Gradually the taste and the pace improved, although he was quite moved by my managing skills and dedication towards him. And one fine day, he popped the most significant question in the utmost casual way.

'Let's get married this December, on the eve of Christmas. I'll inform my mother and also help you convince your folks,' he said it as if everything between us was just fixed and we were around 30 years old.

I stopped while sipping that cupful of green tea, and the entire process of detoxification halted.

'Is this a marriage proposal?' I asked on being surprised.

'You have any doubts?' he smirked.

'Well, it's the blandest way of a marriage proposal, especially where love is the epicentre!'

'Since love is the centre, there's no requirement of antiques,' he looked at me in composure.

'Difficult...it's too soon! My parents wouldn't agree for sure. You are still studying and above all religion will be a spoiler. Bad idea!'

'Bad idea! Huh, Naads?'

'Miss, you seem to be day dreaming, actually evening dreaming, huh?'

I pulled myself from the dialogues and smelled the reality that I was surrounded with. Yes, I was still sitting like stupid amidst Reena's pre-wedding celebration. The weather had turned soothing, partially cloudy, hiding the intensity of the Sun and waiting for the Moon. The musicians played soothing numbers, old classics!

'Miss, can I get your name, please?' asked Rizvi.

I smiled playfully and looked at him. He smiled back since he understood my pun intended at him. 'Oh C'mon! You think I cannot find out,' he said with a smirk, giving out that slight dimple.

'Go ahead,' I encouraged him.

'First agree on a date with me...hmmm...a tea date?'

I kept thinking and was quite tough on him from the time he'd asked. Usually, I am not too difficult if men asked me out and hence I accepted.

'Chef Rizvi?'

'Oh! Ma'am, nobody has ever addressed me in that fashion,' he said on being startled.

'Is that good or bad?'

'It's fantastic!'

'What is your restaurant named?

'The Desi Resto Bar,' he smirked.

'Is Mumbai ingrained in you? Huh?' I asked about being taken aback a bit.

'A little since it led me ahead with my dreams! You must have heard this from many people, but this place has some vibe of vigour. I love it here, although it's a lot of work and crowd and organization but there's magic here!'

Rizvi spoke with all his flamboyance yet with a warmer feeling towards this place that had offered him a lot of opportunities. His feelings were like a bell curve- rising with energy-getting consistent with emotional attachment and sliding down with silence. It seemed he was too passionate about this place.

'See you at The Desi's over your life of tea tomorrow at 10 am?'

'Let me pinch myself,' he said and winked.

Returning to the posh hotel, I had a guest waiting, an unwanted one for sure! There were suddenly too many men in my life. Scott in UK-Tea date with Rizvi-Jonathon in my thoughts- Ronnie snapping back intermittently and Sanjeev at the hotel's lobby!

16

TOO MANY FOR ONE!

Like a gentle-lady, I invited Sanjeev to the hotel's restaurant and spent some time with him. He was never married. However, he was surely in love with a person of his interest, who shared the same Banking firm in Chicago. She was a Japanese but couldn't get married to him since she wanted to spend the rest of her life in Tibet as a monk. She turned indifferent eventually to the worldly ways and by the time Sanjeev proposed her for marriage; she was jolted and had quit Chicago with a last goodbye.

I saw him turning gloomy since he was a little unfortunate in receiving love, and his relationships were always at the brink of break-ups. He looked well-maintained. At 42 when single men usually turn sordid, he was well-kempt and fit, although nothing could trigger any romance in me for this gentleman. Not that I was guilt-stricken about not falling in love with him, but I didn't wish him bad either.

'So, how did you come down to India at this time of the year?'

'I had to attend Reena's wedding and meet my folks.' I assured him that I didn't come down to check on him, and neither was I on the verge of finding grooms.

He smiled slightly and kept his hands on mine that was placed carelessly on the table and said with a lowered tone, 'If you are willing, I can be a good companion!'

I was not surprised at his trial with destiny yet again, and I definitely think he should be rewarded! Uttering nothing, I excused myself and left the potential marital bliss.

Walking down the aisle-like road of the clean-cut Colaba market, I saw the standby shops that had literally no special accessories but superlative costs. The foreigners tried their best to haggle but still the local shopkeepers outsmarted them. I was guessing why any smart person would fall in for stuff so plain like these. Neither was it artistically designed nor handwoven! I marched forward and also noticed the famous Leopold café that witnessed the 26/11 massacre. The café was functioning in its full swing. There was a huge rush for sure, and I have overheard that there were greater possibilities to find the who's who of Bollywood here! I didn't want to waste my time over Bollywood stars- but I pondered how life can be brought back to regular, who would've concluded that 10 years back there was a frightening attack at this very spot! I stood at the stoned paved pathway looking and gazing at the speed the attendants were pushing their energies, bringing in the best food items and serving! So, life becomes regular with time, be it any tragedy in the past.

The Desi's was a sea-facing restaurant that resembled a ship! It was a huge place utilized to the best possible. The deck like area had an open space facing the sea, which was also utilized as a miniature playground for the kids. The inside of the restaurant had a terrific oblong structure that provided a separate counter for food & drinks. It had huge cushion-like seating spaces and lower tables, which made the place an irregular resto-bars I have ever visited! The restaurant was open for tea, coffee, and breakfast in the morning. Overall, it was a quirky but unique place to be at.

'I am looking for Chef Rizvi,' I asked at the reception that had a pretty looking female dressed up like a man.

'Certainly Ma'am! May I have your name please?'

'I am Nayantara Pani.'

The pretty girl at the reception rushed inside, asking me to take a seat of my likeness. Probably, she was used to this; females asking for her boss quite often! All she did during our brief conversation was sheepishly smile.

'How many females visit you in the morning?'

'Believe me, none! That makes you the first in the morning category! Hahaha.'

'I had guessed it! The first time that I had met you.'

'What? That I am flirtatious, huh?'

'Spot on!'

'Tell me something new! I had to live up to your expectations, right?

It was tough to annoy this gentleman! He had a smile to every remark that I threw at him! Nevertheless, it also spoke about his irrevocable perseverance to tolerate people and their judgments, which only few men were born with! I was quite impressed with how he turned the table to a positive one. Not only was he a high energy to be with but he was extremely positive. None will be bored in his company!

As it was almost noon, Rizvi excused himself to have a check on his kitchen. It was imperative for a restaurant owner cum head chef to act and deliver the best quality service to its guests. He seemed extremely passionate about his food and guests as if that's the life he's chosen and he's too submerged in it. I liked that he was passionate about his kitchen.

As Rizvi requested me to relax by the seafront and wait for his delicious Desi delight brunch, I was sipping an exuberant glass of margarita and enjoying the sunny side of life. Looking at the sea, I had wiped off all worries of Scott and its peripheral mess, the single yet wealthy life at Rickmansworth and my hectic mundane work schedule, the past dismissal from Jonathon, to an extent Ronnie and also about my nagging parents, who spoke about nothing but my marriage! I was at ease, in my zone, my space of this free world, ironically at one of India's busiest cities, Mumbai!

I felt exuberant looking at the sea and feeling wonderful.

Exactly at 45 minutes to one, Rizvi sent me another Pinacolada, Desi's special drink, and served it with cheddar cheese and mint salad. I was at some exotic place it seemed, enjoying every sip and bite of my life here! 'Heaven!' I whispered to the sea, sheepishly looking at its sleepy afternoon waves.

'Naads! Oh, Jesus!' shrieked a sorrowful voice.

I woke up from my wonderland and looked at the most impossible encounters in the most ecstatic situation ever!

'Good Lord! You here and why like this?' I questioned since it was the only thing that occurred to me!

'Life struck, Naads but Jesus saved me!'

Jonathon Rodrigues and my life back at the Portuguese haven was like a swift walk in the clouds. Floating, rolling, dreaming, and cuddling each other, we spent almost two years together. Although I didn't permanently live with him, the shuffle was still continuing. The old couples started asking us to get married as soon as it could be possible and give birth to many children. They'd even started fixing the names!

'Let's do it!'

'What? Marriage? It's too early!'

'Absolutely not!'

'it will terrify my parents. And I am not prepared enough to convince them, not yet! You are just a graduate, too young to be married!'

'You should have thought about it before getting committed,

Naads,' Jojo said sternly looking at me.

'You are getting me wrong, Jojo. All I am trying to say is that I need time, and this isn't the right one! Things will be very difficult for us, in terms of marriage. And I am not covering it up with a fairy-tale saga either!'

'You are right, Naads! It isn't a fairy-tale! It's bullshit!'

That night, Jojo didn't return to fetch me up from my place of stay. He had picked his trivial battle with me for reasons of adamancy and not rationalism. It hurt me since I couldn't be callous to my parents either. It's Puri and my relatives would outcast me. Suddenly, my thoughts grew deeper into the cultural upbringing that I've had at Puri and how it would be rough on my part to break the news of marrying a Catholic to my parents! Of-course Jojo was right when he said that these concerns should have bothered me in my days in Goa and not to this day. However, it was difficult explaining to him I was a mere college girl in Goa and a grown-up woman in Bangalore-this transformation made a lot of dissimilarities!

The next day, with the hope of meeting Jonathon, I took a leave quite early and went to meet him at his regular college spot. By meeting a few of his friends, I got an idea that he must be practicing violin back at home since he had a music event lined up this weekend. One of his friends corrected me I might find him at The Christmas Tree Hotel, he had to pick up a gig there. I crossed almost half of the city while trying to reach him. It was a quarter to five in the evening when I found him sloshed at the hotel's bar.

'Is this how you practice for a music event?'

He half-opened his eyes and seemed sloshed, 'You've ruined my life, Naads! I had loved you with all my heart and soul, accepted you entirely with your flaws, had made terms with our cultural difference, your strange beliefs and premonitions, your mood swings and arrogance, tried to bridge the gaps, your constant remarks about our age difference...you choosing Bangalore instead of Goa...I had levelled my thoughts as per your suitability but you turned out to be a traitor to my land of dreams, to our future together, even to us now! You are nothing but a self-centred bitch! And I don't want to mind my language! I loved a bitch! And have been loving you all this while! So, get the hell out of here and out of my sight at once and for all!

His words pricked me hard, though I was quiet at his antics, quiet since he was drunk; knowing that he expressed his buried emotions. I was deeply hurt but didn't react at all. He dramatized things between us by over-reacting. It was very clear from his body language and his sharply chosen words. The staff at the hotel watched me as if I was a distorted object. Their expressions striking and serious, Jonathon was a friend to them, not me! How dare I hurt their friend, their colleague!

I left the hotel in despair, my looks dishevelled, my eyes soared and my throat dry. After almost an hour, I found a bus to commute to my place. I didn't like the entire sequence. The way he misinterpreted the concern for my parents. Still, I didn't want to be crass and ignorant of our relationship. I wanted to allow him time and space. To frame it otherwise, I needed some time to recover.

It was a week we didn't speak to each other in pursuit of our everyday lives. I'd never seen this insensitive side of him, although I'd witnessed his no communication a winter back. I kept hoping that one day he would realize and call. I wasn't being egoistic. I was just being judicious.

Weeks turned into many days. Still no calls. Keeping aside every dams and ditches, I reached for him at his rented place. Reaching the gate, I called again. That evening, walking by the cobbled stone path, alongside the flower pots placed asymmetrically, something awkward struck my mind. I had walked in that lane so often and yet it didn't feel this strange. I rang the bell which seemed to be a classic doorbell. The old Uncle was out, fixing his housecoat and trying to wear his glasses.

'Uncle, hello! I am looking for Jonathon.'

He saw me through his thick glasses and called for his wife, who seemed faster than him.

'Oh, Nayantara! Where have you been all this while? I was

wondering. It's so good to see you. Please come inside,' said and opened the door.

She offered me a cup of chocolate syrup as the winters in Bangalore had embarked.

'Don't be disappointed. Lord always plans greater things in life.' She spoke in the middle of me sipping the delicious chocolate syrup.

'Naads! Why are you so quiet?' Jonathon literally shook me and tapped on the table. 'Listen, I have to go. I work in this place as an Engagement Manager. Keep my business card and call me, please.'

I was extremely composed, which was quite unlikely of me, just nodded with his see-off. Looking around, I found myself in the restaurant and Rizvi onlooking with 'what's up girl!'

'Hey! You met your ex? Am I correct?' he tapped my shoulders.

'Bug off!' I said, trying to ignore him.

'C'mon, Nayantara! Tell me.'

'He's just a man I knew in the past. Not important enough to discuss.'

'I'll believe if you say so… make this man important!' He said it with a wink and a smile.

'Really?'

'You seem pretty nice. Why wouldn't I try my chance…hmmm…. to go to the UK!'

'Just nice, huh? And the UK? Really?'

'Why not!'

I giggled, and he suddenly asked me out another time. This time it was for his stand-up show.

17

Unleashed at Rickmansworth

Elsa's early morning bark made Nelsa whimper. Mrs Patrick came straight running to the living hall where both the hounds were comforting each other. She patted them and took both of them to her lap. After all, both of them were her darlings, her perpetual babies. While doing so, she fell asleep out of the previous night's hectic work of the house and also of Nicola's son. It was a dual-task for Mrs Patrick at this age and at this winter. Nicola was a helping hand for sure, but these days she kept to herself. Wasn't the lively soul that she used to be. She seemed more lost than she was at Leicester.

The sudden thud at the room's door woke up Mrs Patrick, and she muzzled the hounds who shivered by a few seconds. Without paying much attention to the sound of the door, she dozed off on the couch. The door was again unlatched and this time, Elsa was the first to compromise her sleep and go running towards the main door. Mrs Patrick, like a true housekeeper, ran to the shut door and couldn't find anything. It was six-thirty in the morning and she remembered that she had to check on the baby who was sleeping in the guest room.

Adrian was fast asleep, but without Nicola by his side. This irked Mrs Patrick. 'How irresponsible a woman she can be!' With anger, she marched outside the room to glimpse the girl. Alas! Nicola was nowhere to be found in the house. She was slightly vexed since six-thirty isn't a time for her to stroll in the nearby park. Putting on her gloves and overcoat, she tied the leash to her hounds and set for the nearby botanical park.

It was a well-manoeuvred plant hub with a water body to add to its beauty. She usually ventured here to feel the fresh air, dissuade her worries and anxiety in the company of Elsa and Nelsa. Today, she inhaled the fresh yet chilly air of the town, yet admiring its non-material beauty. Had she been a poet, romance would have taken the blue and white for sure. She wished to be a poet, and she remembered Nayantara penning down a few, usually when in pain and solitude. She has had high regards for Nayan- a single woman in a foreign soil having achieved so much yet without any arrogance! 'Miss you Nayan,' she murmured to herself and realized that she was missing her presence. On getting back to her current search spree, she continued looking for Nicola, unleashing the dogs.

'I am tired of this girl now. Her antics are too frivolous for a cultured person like me,' she fumed this time. Sitting by the waterside bench and trying to close her eyes. She heard a voice too familiar.

'I'll visit you next time in the place you stay,' said the man.

'Please no! As it is, I'm too shamed by my act. I'll be disowned. Please don't,' said the female.

'There shouldn't be any. She is an egocentric female who used me. You are a warm woman. You care. And I care for you too!'

Mrs Patrick turned suspicious as both the voices sounded familiar. She tried unravelling the faces to the voices heard. She walked as fast as she could, forgetting about her hounds for a moment. 'Goodness gracious! O Lord!' she saw and uttered in sheer disgrace. With guilt and discredit mounting her head, she was left shell-shocked and immediately left for the house. The hounds followed her.

The mirror, as if cracked; her culture, as if splurged on vulgarity and infamy. She was humiliated. 'Nah...I just can't believe my eyes!'

She sobbed and cursed of mothering a slut-like daughter, Nicola, who was run by her hormones and not by her sanity.

> *'The infamous Us*
> *Entwined between white and grey*
> *With a spray of passion and disregard*
> *Although highly contagious but greatly a farce!*
>
> *The Infamous Us*
> *Laying on top of each other*
> *Sometimes inside…*
> *Although coated with vigour but with shallow talks at par!*
>
> *The Infamous Us*
> *Defamed in Adultery and targeted as Cheats*
> *Are looked down upon*
> *No matter how zealous we may be!*
>
> *The Infamous Us…*
> *Perpetrators of Hope and Love*
> *Trying to bridge gaps of lies!*
>
> *Love-lust it is!*
> *And we are the remnants of it…*
> *-Nayantara'*

Nicola read the poem with a long pause and stillness around her. She could relate to the deep sense of it. Each word was bitter, harsh but added reality to her existence. How has it happened? It was under her control but she let it go as she had always to the demands of passion and loneliness, both criss-crossed, yet kept hoodwinked in the eyes of outsiders. It was not hidden from her that this sexual attire that was worn by her multiple number of times, was her biggest strength and so it was her greatest weakness. She succumbed to the genuineness of it. Nevertheless, it made her anxious since she piled on her hopes of getting back to a sexual bliss with Scott. A man was as mysterious and hibernated as the darkness of her future. Well thought was seriously not in her list of phrases since she had never ever perceived situations as they should have been regularly. It was only she and the desires of her heart in eternal need of romance and attention. All she wanted was a partner in crime who she could present her truest human feelings and shower him with everything man and material.

Nicola was nothing but a Goddess of misfortune. She loved her late husband Daniel with all the intrinsic poise and posture that a man desires in a woman, yet she was this infinite circle of solitary. Her happiness was never a static element. It kept revolving and dipping like her youth. Only career and Adrian couldn't caress her feelings with wonders. She needed more. She needed a man who she could always fall back on, retreat to—emotionally and physically.

'My darling daughter, my only pride, how could you be such a whore?' a voice from behind at its ugliest words but with utmost saddest tones.

'O, mother! I didn't understand the reason for this?'

'I beg of you to go back to Leicester, please. Don't ruin Nayan's life as you have ruined yours. After a long time, she likes someone and tolerates him too. You meddlesome child! Run from here. Save my pride! Save yours' if left. Go from Rickmansworth. From our lives.'

'Scott and I are in love, mother! I shouldn't leave. He'll be hurt,' said Nicola in a sober tone.

'You call that Love! Love? Huh?'

'Love has all forms. Not one is truest, and not one is wrong. Love like the wind which is directionless for the rational mind yet holds on to its own direction. It has no one interpretation. It's as per a living creature's suitability, ability to understand. Love is polygonal and only its complexities enriches human experiences.'

Mrs Patrick slammed the living room door and was in disgust. She reprimands, but nothing prevails. What prevails is the residual shame that her daughter has put her at. Terrible is her state of mind these days as she sees the lust-prone ongoing between Scott-the unforeseen and her daughter- the impulsive.

'Fire & Ice never collide
When it does, it gets onto a stride
The stride is a convoluted maze
Puzzling, mettlesome yet spirits at a peaceful haze!

Waking and breaking is a blithering fable here,
Stops and pauses run side by side dear!
Yet it sings the mushy tunes in denial,
Meandering through the zippy tales of burial!

Fire & Ice together, a seductive piece,
Where earth seeks the hilltop peace
This foregoing tale of oddity…
Though has an end to its perpetuity
But will be entwined till eternity.
-Nayantara'

A few weeks in Rickmansworth has proven fatal. Attraction has to pay a price. Hence, without informing Scott, and on-demand from her mother, Nicole left alone, without Adrian by her side; to her destined place—Leicester. As Nicola took the train back to her town, her heart pounded heavily. She sighed for a moment, thinking love was never meant to be hers. She was as if an outcast in the matters of relationships, but her lustful heart never stops desiring. And this time it was raging for Scott. The train journey unfolded a lot of musings of the craving mind. She was undoubtedly restless, and only her mother was to be blamed. Adrian was her only person around, but even he was kept away from her company!

Nicole was sent to Leicester to work at a privately owned College Library. She was disgusted with the way things turned out, although ashamed of her untrustworthy behaviour with her employer, nevertheless she found her man, her passions with Scott. She liked these thrills so much that she wanted to dedicate her life to it. The doors which were forbidden, she liked to trespass and how!

With Scott's memory, she reached Leicester. She had a haven, a smaller one, and could not plan her longings alone there. 'O mother!

Why did you put me in exile?' She loved her mother and owed it to her, hence questioning her decision was out of her system, not a ritual she could practice. Nevertheless, the promise made to her mother on not calling up Scott seemed far-fetched. She desired Scott, his body, his physical being, his scent, his cravings, his warmth, and she was not in denial of it. But she couldn't decide when to break this news. When to call it out that she exited out of Rickmansworth. She was a religious being and believed that the new year would bestow her with things of her want; that she would again unleash her true spirits, live and be the way that she wants to be! Hence, she waited...

18

STOP BY THE LIBRARY

The Brookshire Library's assistant job was not at all an easy piece of cake to walk with. It was a lot more demanding than she thought it would be. She spent more time in the library than her tiny house. It was a 10-hour job that paid her 1800 pounds per month and was extremely empowering. No sooner, she kept her sexual needs at bay, forgetting the torrid affair with Scott at Rickmansworth.

It was several weeks and Scott was a matter of the lost times to her now, although undeniably she pondered about him when she retired to bed. She recalls her passionate moments with him now and then. Though she feels like a mixed bag-a mother seeking a burning passion. She misses Adrian by her side and she couldn't figure out who she missed the most, Scott on top of her or Adrian by the side of her bed. But for once, she had been strong and not frail, to be what she had never been in her life-decisive!

That day, while she was working on the history book section, she found a book that said, 'I, the Country-Woman of India, it got her attention and all this while she had never really been a book person. But something caught her this time. She issued the book in her name and was charged a barely minimal amount since she was an employee of this huge college library. That night she read about Queen of Jhansi, Freedom fighter Sarojini Naidu, women's army of Azad Hind Force, and many such tales that stirred some hormones of extremities.

> *'To be or not to be*
> *What is meant to be or not…*
> *It's a funny game out here…*
> *Even if you try to blend…*
> *It'll create a pit of fire*
> *If you don't*
> *The burial is anyways ready!*
> *-Nayantara'*

It was a new emotion for her since she knew only stimulation of the sexual body. That night was a first-time revelation to a new world of adventure and soundness. Nicola had always been a hopeless romantic, never a stirred philosopher, that night something had changed. With that book and Nayantara's manuscript, she got entangled or rather forayed into a new world of experiences---the world of thinkers--

'Should I be an emotion, I would've run down your spine, veins, and the indecisive heart, to make you realize how intense of an affair I could be!' The quote was hopeless yet extremely mushy, it jittered me, as if throwing me back to my yesteryears of romance at Goa. It was beautifully wrapped in a shiny red cloth, with bows smiling back at me.

Sometimes first impressions wrong you vehemently and that wrongdoing is hurtful but this time it was a cause of merry-making. Rizvi's short and crisp die-to-be-with-you romantic quote just caught me in the morning. I was already boarding for Bhubaneswar since Puri didn't have a direct flight. Yet I had decided that Rizvi's happy-go-lucky nature is not at all far-fetched. It's easily attainable. He is so vibrant inside that it reflects on the outside. His state of happiness isn't inter-dependent on external factors and that's what has inspired me to meet him again. And the schedule of my trip just got hazed up by many weeks. Instead of Puri, I was forced to stay in Belgaum and Kerala—the Reena effect. She had got the itinerary ready even without informing me. More than her honeymoon, it was our friendly outing together, with her super-rich family to my comfort all the time. My parents were furious over the phone!

The homecoming, after two long years, was different. I was calmer, composed and much contended in life. I knew about the awkward questions and was prepared for it. This time, I didn't think of any answers since I chose not to. This time I wanted to pose like a stout tree, taking the horrific storm, the sultry dry heat, yet standing tall, standing like me, robust and resilient. Yes! It was me! Resilient is what I am.

Exchanging my number with Rizvi was a boon and also a bane! He seemed moonstruck! He kept texting me in and out of the day I landed in Puri. It was, as if, I had a constant somebody crazily into me! After all this year, that feeling of answering someone constantly seemed too much of a liability to me. I didn't know how to turn him down…at least for messages. I liked his company but not when I am doing my own work! And strangely, I had ditched Jojo's offer to visit his place since I had a flight to catch. And it bothered me as I had met him just out of the blue, unexpected, like a huge door-slamming across my face. It was harsh on God's part to just throw people at me, people from the past who I don't want to meet or greet ever.

In the midst of my thoughts, I heard a knock on my door to visit the nearby flea market that seemed to be a weekly one with seashells, conch shells on sale, with locally made decorative pieces. To my mother, I was still 20 years old.

'Buli, I am 63 years old now, knees pain while taking the stairs and trying to squat. I had cataract surgery last year. Although, you had booked the hospital but never cared to attend to me in person. You are my only child and you find no time for me. I am still your mother,' she said and took out the end of her starched cotton sari to wipe off her tears. She sobbed, and it was difficult to see her cry.

Although embracing her would have been ideal, but I was uncomfortable in actioning that…there was something strange, not about my mother sobbing but about me embracing her. It has been two years since I visited my folks, and this gap had probably left me uncaring. Although I wanted to just calm her down, offer her my warm touch, but I was hesitant and I just sat facing the huge sea snarling at me, and listen to my mother weeping intermittently with how much of a stony affair I had become in the west; how the material had engulfed the emotion in me. Nonetheless, not every bit was true. I wasn't emotionless. I had never prioritized money over the heart, it was just that I couldn't advocate my emotions, couldn't float it through my speech. I failed in consoling my mother, who had very caringly brought me up through the perils of life. The journey back home was quieter than I thought. My mother was graver and thoughtful. It was bothering me to the core. My mind spoke so many words that night.

I was sleepless due to my irregularities in expressing gratitude and wording love for my folks. It was truly a night where extreme emotions needed to be expressed but due to the distance, the gaps of undermining each other's plausible acceptance, I kept things inside of me. Although, I wanted to rush to my parents' bedroom and give my mother a sheer embrace, sleep beside her, play with her cotton sari's end, tell her stories of Rickmansworth, tell her I had given a piece of me to a few men in the west and also that most men around the globe had the same genetic coding!

A mother who is considered supreme in our books of history and mythology can only understand these unspoken dealings of the heart; who is nature and also natural, who is the creator and also creative, who is love and also lovely, who is heaven and also home! I got out of my bed since my mind was wandering with all lineless directions. Reaching the threshold of the balcony made me see life, my life from a distance. I used to do the same at my place in Rickmansworth, stand along with the window, and look at the street. For all the reasons, I get that we are individuals, with tastes, beliefs, lifestyle, and food to our choice, however, companionship is never harmful, never a bad choice. Be it in the form of a parent, a partner, a friend, a pet, or just a house caretaker, we all, no matter how practical we say we are, would always be glad to walk into a house with somebody waiting for us, caring for us or complaining to us. We all need that somebody…actually everybody needs a somebody…

'Everybody needs a Somebody…

In the meddlesome glory called life,
Where every angle of possibility is stifling…
Be it microorganisms, be it the divinity or the meagre humanity,
All of us are Everybody!

That Everybody, if left alone, will brood in the dark and shiver in callous,
Tryst will take over triumph and power will retreat in a negative halo!

Hence, "besides" is a delightful connotation here, where Everybody has a Somebody!
This befitting entwining of the soul will make the Sun gay, the Sky high and the ink-blue Ocean sigh!

Inferring from the sand of times,
Everybody needs a Somebody, to turn this existence into blissful profundity!'

The morning was warmer than usual, probably due to my monthly cycle. At around 40, the nature of periods is different and non-messier than in the teens or twenties! I have had a gynaecologist in the UK who'd asked me to conceive before I turned 34, since it reduces the risk of having a healthy child. By then, I wasn't used to sex or men, nor did I crave for a relationship, a partner who would willingly collaborate with me to carry his child. I was effervescent, vibrant and indulged in work, everything and anything centred on my work. Nah…not just money but sheer pleasure of doing work. The doc had explained to me how the efficiency of the female egg reduces when a woman turns 30 and that it's always advisable to carry a baby pre-that age. And that there is a biological clock that affects the women post 30. The doc's concerns were respected; however, I had questioned him one thing that he didn't have an answer to.

'Doc, if women post 30 become non-productive and create

inefficient eggs, why do we still have a menstrual cycle, why do the eggs still rupture when there's no union of the sperm? Why do we still have the same cramps, same sensitivity in the bowel and feel nauseous like we felt when we were mere 19! Why do we still produce eggs? Why don't we have menopause just at 30! Why do some women still reproduce children after 30? And why do some fail before they turn 30!'

The doc was a gentleman, and he had got up from his seat like a gust of wind, and sat in front of me, holding my hands and stating, 'I am sure you'll have beautiful babies with a mind of their own!'

'Well…not too sure of that, doc!'

The morning breakfast was followed by a trip to Satapada, a spot where Irrawaddy Dolphins were famously spotted. I remember having ventured twice during my childhood, with the fascination of taking pictures with a few. One was a school picnic, and another was a family outing. Both trips, although joyful, however, had left me quite jittered. The dolphins must be petrified, by so many of our race, without seeking their permission, just stepping into their safe havens, must be so shocking to them! I had pondered then…however, my father had corrected my concerns by stating that they were well-protected to which I had just merely nodded.

Even today, my concern was similar regardless of whether or not some Act preserves them. I saw my mother displaying her pale pink sari with the diamond pendant that I had gifted her. Although wrinkled, she still possessed the beauty of the East Indian girl. Age had defined her beauty, I felt, and yoga had brought her back into shape. Comparatively, my father was looking older and restless than her. Post-retirement, he had been impatient and agitated at things of mere nature. Be it a delay in getting the meal made or the gardener unable to trim the plants accurately. He seemed to be agitated at every odd and even thing in life. Being old was not his dilemma, but being jobless was. He had succumbed to time-bound stuff like never. He fired the maid who didn't bring him tea on time, the newspaper guy who flung the newspaper in the portico than the threshold of the gate, the janitor who didn't seem to dress properly, the laundry guy who was a day delayed with this service…and the list went on! My dad listened to nobody except being held liable for misbehaving with fellow human beings in the land where Lord Jaganath ruled! Yes! It was a bait used to calm him down. And it pricked me in an extremely funny manner what level of trust did he carry for his favourite deity. I now got a hang of this! An art to deal with my jobless father!

> *'You had promised to return: returned only the Rain,*
> *You had promised to carve me on your soul: carved was only said,*
> *You had promised to not demarcate Love: demarcation is what you left,*
> *You had promised to offer a ring: Offered was I negligence,*
> *You had promised to hold my hands: Held was I in your prison,*
> *You had promised to look into my eyes: Looks of despair was put across,*
> *You had promised to kiss my forehead: kiss of banishment was I gifted,*
> *You had promised to return: returned only the echo of my thoughts…*
> *You are a Man with mere promises… and distance is what you shall be bestowed upon!*
> *--Nayantara'*

A tear or two rolled down across Nicola's fragile neck. She was put into the expulsion of her thoughts. Nayantara's heartful work was affecting her as a person. Yes! She had returned from Rickmansworth with a record of her poems, and while typing it out, it had spaced her out into philosophy and life.

She missed Scott, in extremities of her emotions. However, she had decided not to present herself with him anymore. She had visions about her future, and that future only had Adrian's well-being. She was ready to play a warm mother and a strong father. With much difficulty, she had her sexual desires curbed, not cured. Somebody from the library had directed her to a sex shop, and had told her that where a man can't perform, these gadgets can! She was completely thrown off the rack but gradually decided to visit the store.

Ghastly visuals, she discovered in that store, which was in a secluded alley of Norman lane, where strange people landed. The first visit was surely a shocker. The second was fruitful. It was almost three months that she was all by herself, working hard, saving money and putting her needs to the ditch. The shopkeeper was keen in her non-interested and shocking expressions. She picked up a catalogue and directed her to a weird-looking device saying, 'Take this one, it hurts less, feels as little as itchy, but is a tremendous workforce. However, goods once sold are never returned! It's only 5.99 pounds. It reaches like no man!'

Nicola was almost on the ground when she heard that. She was a sexual creature for sure, but she had never depended on a mere gadget for sex. She returned the catalogue to the shopkeeper and said, 'A man understands love, this mere device doesn't!' On her return, she presented her visiting card to the shopkeeper and invited her over to the Brookshire library's annual auction to be held in the next week, stating that there will be a clearance sale too!

'Please stop by the library this weekend. Unlike these gadgets, there are books. And a book takes you through all veins of emotions…'

19

BEYOND MOONLIT NIGHT

Borivali's Kirloskar Residency was probably not at all witnessed to Jonathon's effervescent playing of the guitar or the Cello, not to forget the magical tear-dropping tunes through his violin. The meagre condition at which these godly pieces were stacked in the rack was a mere disappointment. More so, he seldom cared! He was very much a hospitality man now. The apartment was a depiction of how mediocrity had settled at some places in Mumbai. At once, Mumbai was a lavish city of the rich and at the other it was also a city of poverty-stricken people and not to forget one of the best examples of the great Indian middle-class. Such disparity and such contradictions were disturbing to me. However, such was the case with developing nations; where you find all kinds of world boxed into one piece of earth; where food, clothing & shelter still took precedence and where money always existed in the by lane of struggle.

My predicament was unsettled as I had imagined a better and brighter future for Jonathon, while we were in love, back in Goa. I'd never even after the messy break-up, imagined that he would reconcile with something like this. His musical extravaganza was wrapped in some concrete missionary shelve, untidy and locked…uncared for!

'Would you like coffee or tea? Or probably beer would do?'

'I'll be fine with tea. Thanks!'

I tried adjusting myself to his tiny yet cosy apartment, where the horrific sight of the musical instruments kept lurking at me. I tried to dissuade my attention to the neatly placed book rack-I saw a book that read Rumi, and my eyes were hooked onto that.

My love for poetry was undisclosed to people close to me. My most favourite poet is John Keats' 'To Autumn'. I'd found the book at my school library when out of compulsion in the library period, my Literature teacher, out of directives, had asked me and a few other folks to not waste time, snapping back at each other over mere school seniors but read something substantial...she took us to the library, we were some 10 odd people, wasting our time doing nothing but ogling at the nothingness of human bodies; she randomly picked 10 books from the shelf that read Prose & Verse! After a few minutes of unwanted energy in that room, I received, 'To Autumn" by John Keats. Never did I imagine that it would embark on a new journey for me; where I would explore a poet in me.

'You like Rumi?'

'Can't say but I've come across a few of his quotes, which are quite intriguing since they are true!'

'I never knew you liked poetry! Revelation...'

'I expect only me to understand me!'

He grinned and offered me the tea. 'Sorry, the house is a little messy, as my kids are nothing but two hooligans!'

'How old are they?'

'Freddy is 8 and Nyle is 6.'

I saw him blush heartily when he uttered his children's names. I understood that the passion for music had been taken over by the love of the offspring so much that those mesmerizing instruments that produced evangelical percussion had vanished. It was shocking to me since my last visit to London's Imperial music festival, I'd encountered many parents who'd not given up music for any challenges that life posed to them. Their passion superseded the mere wants of life…they managed music and parenthood so well. I had admired their undying aspiration. But I somehow feel we overact, over-explain, over-do things that are not required.

'Don't you play anymore?' I asked since I was thinking of asking him.

'Not really,' he said and put his saucer on the coffee table.

'I don't see your wife. Does she work during Sundays?'

'No, she doesn't. She's out to her Aunt's place.'

There was a very odd silence between us. I was done with the tea and felt as if there was nothing more to be discussed. I smirked. It was forced. He understood.

'Alright, I thought I would meet your family but bad luck. I have to make a move since I have to make a call. Thanks for inviting me over.'

'Hey! You are most welcome! I am sure my family would have loved to meet you. And you can keep that book.'

'This! Are you sure?'

'Why not! Consider it as my gift for you,' he grinned and opened his arms to probably embrace me.

'Hold! Not needed! As far as the book is concerned, thanks a lot!'

'Why are you so indifferent, Naads? Will you never forgive me? It's ages now! I have repented and have written so many letters to you. Anger isn't a great emotion to carry forward. Look, for my actions, we are not together, for my silly act of negligence, I am doing a job just to carry on with my life! My life…music…instruments…all shattered into a bombarded corner of my brain. I have literally lost things that I valued the most. You have proved your point like I did many years back. I was younger, vulnerable but not to this day!'

'I have realized after you left for the UK, what a star you were! So genuine and so honest! I value us, Naads. I value our well-spent youth in Goa. I value all the songs I'd written in our memory, the road trips in Margao, Panjim; the sun-tanned bath in the sea, me baking for you; your scintillating touch, our Bangalore journeys; the complexities; I have it all ingrained with me…probably I'll take it with me to my grave. Also, I notice you not addressing me as Jojo but taking my full name and I completely understand you, your notions, your maturity, your responsibility. Trust me or not, I still regard you as the love of my life! Maybe it's too heavy and child-like to hear me say all this, but why not! Today, after almost two decades, I am professing something so deeply buried inside of me, which has almost given me shuddering nightmares all this time…'

'And you ask me the reason for the musical instruments being piled up like mere logs of wood, it's because of my decision to not sing…not play…no Nayantara…no music…no life!' as he uttered the few last lines, he slouched on the sofa, placed a little next to the book shelf, and seemed very shaky.

I was silent as he spoke, allowing him to blurt out his anguish. Knowing that he had lost quite a lot of his favourite things in life, and that he's repenting, I walked up to him and placed my hands on his head, which was buried in his palms.

'Hey! We all screw up, which makes us the biggest assholes on earth, but what circles it back is that we realize; repent and fall down… but only to rise better! If you have considered me as the 'love of your life', make sure those musical magical rides ain't lost in the man-made shambles! Take them out…play them…they are alive…they'll love you back…you'll soon have fresh and brilliant memories! Your kids will go crazy for you, so will your wife! Play for yourself. Play for them! Rejuvenate your life, Jojo!'

He suddenly looked up, straight into my eyes, and held my hands tightly and wept like a baby!

'He walked beyond the Moonlit night

Shuddering his pride, climbing to its stride

Vexed and vulgar, skipping human self

He strutted like an unruly creature

Intoxicated with colourful potions

Yelling with darker spirits pride

He walked beyond the Moonlit night

Only to be thrown into black and high tide

He was washed against the rough shores

That hurt his physical temple and fused mind

Only when the light was dim and the breathing almost gone

He faced the Moonlit night…

Smirked the Moon and said, 'you had walked beyond me all this while, what you thought gold was a faceless dime! Until you fall, you could've seldom realized!

--Nayantara'

Nicola almost hit the floor hard when she read the last monologue by the Moon, which can be interpreted either as your conscious or your constant intelligent mind; or some cosmic voice representing your inner voice. She reread the last sentence yet again and was deeply remorseful because one has to fall hard to realize. She could relate the poem to her situation.

That day she left early from work. Nayantara's intriguing verse was making her restless. She could almost read in-between lines. She could feel it to be her…the sinful acts, the guilt lane and now being lonely. She headed yet again to the alley where a few women travelled- the Norman lane.

'What a pleasant surprise!' greeted the same storekeeper.

'Hi, I am not here for what you are thinking. I am here to find out a thing of my relevance.'

'Lady, we don't judge our customers…potential customers too!' she smiled and said gently.

'I am not looking for a sex toy or any adult product. I just wanted to talk to you!'

The storekeeper never delved into a conversation of this nature. She was literally puzzled.

'Don't look dazed! I am just here to talk to you! Since out of the thousand illicit relationships and not a single friendship in this town, I only know you, in this amazing shop of sex-dwellers. People at the library are damn serious to talk! They only read. It's not that I don't read but I have no friends…what a fucking life I have been living… like literally…there's nobody to talk to! Men who slept with me; only prefer to sleep with me rather than indulge in simple talking! They are not to be blamed; probably I only featured myself like that. I am a fool! Isn't it? I don't even know your name!'

'I am Bella Johnson from Holland. I came to England with my dear husband a decade back.'

'Hey, Bella! I am Nicola Patrick. I am a widow. My late husband was serving in the UN armed forces. He was killed in a bomb blast. I still love him. I have a son named Adrian and I have a lovely mother, who wouldn't look at my face for my immature deeds. And I work at the Brookshire Library after having dwelled into a preposterous act in Rickmansworth, where my mother works.'

'O dear! Who knows what a sin is…it's all so relative in here! And you are no fool since only diligent people realize their mistakes and not fools in actuality. So, nice meeting you Nicola!'

'Thanks for catching up! You can call me Nicole.'

''Well…then…Nicole it is.'

'I am full of guilt and crap. I think I am a very bad and selfish person.'

'Listen to me dear, go to your place, let's meet tomorrow, after work. Okay? And take this little piece of fun, it'll make you laugh!'

Nicola paid five pounds for some little wonder that Bella had finally sold to her.

'Like hell, it's a replica of a miniature man with an erect penis and when you pinch on the tip, it screams, 'Baby don't prick since I am your man…though small in size but a huge heart!' Nicola couldn't contain her laughter at this silly piece of creation. She kept on pinching the tiny man's penis till it ran out of battery. That night she cried in laughter, that night her eyes watered in tears of happiness! A small, silly toy could bring so much of her peppy nights back; she'd never imagined! She thanked Bella a million times. Thought friendship was so much cooler and joyful than sex!

Finally, she saw the moonlit beyond the darkness of the night through a barely known stranger friend and a silly miniature toy!

20

At Bangalore's End!

On leaving behind the old Portuguese style house, which had become our little haven, too many emotions kept drifting and also crossing my path that day. Bidding the old couple, a goodbye was not imagined, neither did I ponder about the perpetual difference between Jojo and me. It was a reality which was an absolute tear-jerker.

I was berserk to hear from the old Aunt that Jonathon had suddenly packed his bags for somewhere…that which he didn't reveal…some solo excursion, where he wanted peace! With that chocolate syrup trying to bear this distasteful truth about my boyfriend, who was submissively seeking peace and not my company was absolute horror! And then he talked about marriage with me, one silly fight and he calls it off, he puffs every sweetness that we had experienced into thin air, he flees like the coward fly! Wasn't he the one ranting about marriage? Wasn't he the guy to be wanting to hear the wedding bells ring? Didn't he just repeat history? He fled this time, last time, he cut-off with no prior communication! Was he just fucking around with my mind? Which part of my story was true? This screwed-up part, or the jazzed romance at Goa? As I walked past the house, my brain started freaking me out with thoughts out of my vulnerable emotion. I was anxious, nervous, heartbroken, mind-fucked, and agitated; all of these at the same time.

Nothing can be worse than a distasteful romance! It will neither let you forget the person nor will it let you hate him…dejections and disappointment ran through my veins. I kept moaning about Jonathon! We were simple and great together! But I think simplicity just threw itself outside the door. He made things complex! We could've talked… discussed. How could he abandon me? Marriage is a stage of life where you want things to be right, orderly, and very much in place. So, what's wrong if I double-checked with my commitment and time! What's so imperative to get married in a rush! It can wait. I am 26 and highly aspirational. Achievements and career are my priority right now, plus I just can't outcast myself. Didn't he know this! He was well informed that my folks would need more time to gulp this side of me. I am their only daughter and I just can't move ahead without their consent!

'There might be an opportunity but outside India,' said my manager, who seemed completely clueless and dazed with my question. 'But Nayan, my question is it's just two years in this location, which was of your choice, although I am subtracting two months of training at Mumbai; don't you think you are yet to explore banking operations in this place. Let me assure you that Bangalore in the coming years will be a hub for jobs and will be bustling with young people. And you want to leave this place?'

'Vijay Sir, I completely agree with you but I just don't like it here anymore. Send me to Bhubaneswar or Delhi. Mumbai is too expensive and crowded. Am I sounding too demanding?'

'No, Nayan! Absolutely not! You seem distressed. Probably some things are not as per planned. But does that mean, we change the course of our lives? Huh? You are doing well and you've graduated from one of the premier business schools! But again…I'll not try to judge you. You understand your situation better. Still, Indian location shifts might be a problem. I can help you go outside India, think, and get back!'

'Thanks for understanding!'

That weekend post-work, a couple of work friends wanted to relax in a nearby social pub which was brand new to the Koramangala area! They dragged me in since I had two of my stupid roommates, who pulled me into anything and everything these days.

Almost half of the white-collared employees were seen to be bustling with joy in these social pubs. Here the décor was something different. The interiors had bricks with white paint, bookshelves, record labels on walls. Colourful lamps hung and the entire place was lighted up with the flowing exuberant energies that people offered. Nobody had a sunken face! It seems everybody with a foul mood or a tiring day, got themselves rid of everything bothering them. Such was the music and energy of this place. It was almost two months that Jonathon Rodrigues had fled and like a bug in my poetry book, his memories kept biting me.

'Nayan, meet Willy!' said a super sloshed Mukti.

'Hey! Willy, have we met?'

'Now we do! Actually, I am a co-owner of this pub with Jaggi and Rudy. And I met this wonderful friend of yours last week and ever since she's been introducing me to her friends! But I like her no-inhibitions attitude towards life. She seems free-spirited, although quite under the spell of the magical potion. Hahaa.'

'True, she seems to be on some gala ride today and probably has been.'

Sadly, when I was in a relationship with Jonathon, I'd missed these crazy yet funny nuances of my great roommates. They were utterly silly but fabulous people to find at work. Whatever little time I had spent with them, I had never prioritized their interests or events over mine. It's a pity on me. Sometimes, we get so immersed in one person that we forget to be inclusive about the rest of the people- for people in it, it's ordinary but in actuality it sucks. You mustn't dedicate your entire existence to only one ongoing-it becomes the most static part of us-the most redundant of all.

Until this night, I had never observed how nice my roommates were! Energetic, easy-going, and fun company. These fortunate occurrences that I'd missed in Bangalore for running after a directionless wind, made me sulk even more. But whatever time I am here, I'll make it noteworthy. I'll be there for these folks and pull myself out of this Jojo-mess! Bangalore, till its end will be a life to remember. I swear on my energies. These shitty affairs lead us nowhere! Where most people just love themselves and pretend to love others-these kinds are nothing but escapists! Mere escapists…let life screw them up! Let them repay their own karma, own up someday, to their own actions! Let them…

The Social Pub became one of the most visited places for us. We danced like psychos, got sloshed like the horse, and talked like it was our last day on planet earth! Movies, shopping with credit cards, missing out on electricity bills, using neighbour's utility for a couple of days, buying a second-hand washing machine, refrigerator, television, we had all the ample necessities of life. Gradually my life had returned to normal, where I had vehemently pushed Jonathon to a corner of the brain where all negative and learning memories were placed-not fond memories for sure. I was glad to do so. It added some kind of strength in me as if I could avoid complexities in life. I felt good about myself. I had seen my friends over these years to sulk, weep, and get depressed in their break-ups but thankfully I was not setting a bad example for anybody or for myself. Definitely, it unnerved that Jonathon wasn't a part of my life anymore; that all my couple goals in life were shattered because of his escapism; and also, that I could've saved my energy and time and love for somebody better than him! But my learning curve in life was steep enough for me to also address that broken relationships makes you headstrong in life; it prepares you… well not to make those mistakes in the next one! Plus, break-up doesn't necessarily mean being ruthless! It just means being learned and wise; a bit matured!

Vijay Nambiar was kind enough to keep my requests in mind. He was a blessing in disguise. Very few bosses must be as progressive and secure like him! He was of settled mind, firm, and an absolute supporter of an effective working style. He cribbed less and channelized more!

His mantra was solutioning or finding alternatives to a situation; and how best must we tackle! He was one of those dynamic minds who was very rare in the bank! Most of us adored him.

'So, Nayan, how are you today?'

'Good, Sir,' I said with a smile.

'Oh! You smile!'

'C'mon Sir! I do a lot many times.'

'Cool! So, there's an opportunity in the UK and also in Manila. In India, there's a tough competition, since internally locals are preferred than any other. It means you stand less chance in our country but have a great chance outside. Both Manila and London are looking for an opening that's matching your profile. Apply for the interview. Let them screen you! If you get selected, it'll be a hell of an opportunity where you can only see ahead. Think. Decide. Keep in mind the dynamics. Act!'

'Hmmm…'

'Don't hmmm, Nayan! We all want to fly! Consider this as your chance to win wings!'

'Thank you, Sir! When do I get back to you?'

'Who needs to move out?'

'Me.'

'So, the sooner the better,' he said and got into a conference call where I kept gazing at him with no interruption.

Getting selected for both the locations outside India was no doubt a sense of achievement to me. Nevertheless, it was worrisome for my folks as I would venture out of the country, where neither they nor I know anybody! Such was my plight that within, I was trying to convince myself a better place to choose and, on the outside, I was convincing both of them I'll be fine. Here, my cousin in Delhi came into the picture, who was just married and was trying to juggle between work transfer and marriage. She helped me a lot in making my parents understand that I will manage things on my own, irrespective of the place. And that marriage is just a part of life, not the wholesome experience of life. After a debate and discussion for over a month, my parents allowed me to go to the UK and not Manila since it was not the UK. Finally, a new place, a new country altogether!

Desi's evening was a very classy affair. Not to forget the effervescent and believer of style, Rizvi, who did everything perfectly for the socialites to go gaga over his event. Yes! I'd revisited Mumbai for Rizvi's event and also met Jonathon consciously. Post Mumbai, the plan was to go back to Puri and take my parents along with me to Rickmansworth. It'll be their second visit to the UK. Things were getting settled down. This trip was more recovering and relaxing than all the previous ones I've had. More because my parents had accepted my way of living without further probing into it. They had somehow organized their traditional mind without being fussy about a husband and children. This was very endearing to me; to have my folks not nagging about me getting married just to anyone.

'How can I thank you, Naads?'

'By offering me a glass of wine,' I said with a smile, looking at Jonathan.

There he was again with his play-master skilful self. I patted my back since I had changed somebody's drowning music life. 'Look at him, just within a fortnight, he returned to life!'

He valued aspiration, his aspiration in music. Although in a small but effective beginning, he had channelized his musical events at The Desi's. Rizvi had been extremely helpful, though. He said that it was crowd-pulling and cost-effective to have someone from the team to enact! Jonathon had learned that life is all about taking leaps and living the moments. He seemed ecstatic and obliged but during all of this…his eyes sparkled with the round of applause…he finally discovered his retreat; won himself back…his music back! And Jojo was never uttered before the new Jonathon.

21

BEHIND ME

Nicola and Bella, although with a huge age difference, had bonded so well that a weekly coffee/tea meeting was bound to take place. Nicola preferred the tiny roadside coffee joints since it was better than her haven. She avoided taking Bella to her tiny one-bedroom apartment since it was not proper. She was embarrassed by her partial mediocrity. Bella because of her wisdom had sensed this side of her and hence she didn't impose much.

On a wintery Sunday, Nicola was invited for an afternoon meal at a picnic spot next to Bella's. She appropriately packed cookies, egg salad, and chocolate mud pie for the picnic. It was exciting since it reminded her of her golden years at school. It took her back to Zen years where her father was alive and her mother was this multitasker humanoid who did almost everything. She baked really well and her favourite being macaroons since it was her father's favourite too! Nicola was, from all senses, his dad's girl. Adored, pampered, and forgiven easily.

She remembered how once she had spoiled the record documents of her mother's mountaineering trekkers, which had upped the anger of Mrs Patrick. Although a dear daughter, she was ready to send her to a boarding school in France for her obstinate behaviour. Gustav, who believed that she'll not mess with her mother's work again, saved her! Mrs Patrick didn't communicate with her for the next so many days until Gustav again intervened and played a moderator.

The memory about her childhood also reminded her of the utmost confidence that Gustav had on her; on her graduating with arts and literature major credits. Since he was a mountaineer, he was wishful that her daughter would pen his excursions, journeys, and expedition to these snow-capped beauties, valuing life, facing death, everything will be penned by Nicola Gustav, his pride!

A tear, invaluable, rolled down her cheeks. As she looked around her tiny house, she found a meagre bed, a side table with a reading lamp, a foyer to the door where books and Nayantara's unpublished poems were arranged neatly. A coat-stand. A faded wallpaper, where a picture of her family was hung with much difficulty, and a tiny wardrobe where few of her non-lavish clothes and necessary things were kept. A bathroom that was the only place that had a mirror, an irregularly small kitchen which stored bare things for a living.

Ponderous and crestfallen, she slouched on the bed. 'What greatness have I achieved in life for my folks to be proud of me…a bland nothing! I was their princess. I am Gustav and Gustavia's only daughter, who achieved heights when they were young. They travelled around the world, helped people, cared for the living creatures around! My mother, at this age, maintains her loyalty, her sanity, her philosophy…what the hell did I learn! I kept fucking up things…I slept with her employer's boyfriend! I am a whore of the highest order.' As she uttered things that were pricking her humanhood, she made a strong decision to confess her bad doings to Nayantara and ask for forgiveness. So was she ready to face her mother, who was of prime importance to her. With firmness in her eyes, she decided to visit Rickmansworth and offer her wrongness for any punishment in store. To allow her mother to order her anything that she wants her to do, in-order to compensate for the fuck-ups that she did. Yes! She was ready to face her lessons.

Realizing that she was getting late to Bella's invitation, she wiped off her tears to her frequently saddened face and dabbed some foundation to look presentable. 'It's only I, who can fix it!'

Bella and her husband Jeffrey were an old yet extremely lively couple. Jeffrey often made fun of Bella's sex shop and the customers that would stop by with their unusual sexual attempts and desires. Some were so blown away by the performance by just looking at a dildo that Bella found it difficult to contain her grin. But she also understood the need for it for people who bought it. Some wanted to explore the realm of desire, a few just for fun, and others for the hype of it. With that laughter and slight sunny rays, Nicola's mud cake was a discovery of her as a great baker. She was applauded for her efforts of making something so delightful that not a bit of it was left in the box.

'Oh! I was too nervous thinking that wouldn't be baked properly.'

'Ahh… common, dear! Too modest you are! Taste this Sauvignon now! Cheers to goodness!'

Also present were her husband's friends with their two sons and a daughter. The picnic mat was insufficient for everybody to rest hence, very courteously, Nicola took the nearby park bench.

They were happy, and she enjoyed every bit of the vibrant thoroughfare that these guys bought in. That partially sunny, partially windy Sunday morning was her transcending story. Unfolding her strength and trying to face her fears. She also realized that she hardly valued such togetherness earlier; that she was nothing but a cock-chaser! She reprimanded her past and tried to create a long-distance of coldness with it!

The next day, she applied for a week's leave from work. It was tougher than she had anticipated. In a library, she never thought her request of leave would take so many rounds, she was flabbergasted at this but made her intentions clear with the owners. They finally agreed and no sooner she made her way to Rickmansworth from where she was asked to leave. It was after so many weeks, nearly seven, that she would meet her mother, Adrian, and the two beautiful hounds. Never did she imagine that she could emulate some ethics of living into her life. This time, she felt a streak of pride about how she could manage what she was and what she is turning into! That brought her relief!

The fencing hadn't changed, neither the lampposts nor the botanical garden or the street carving! She rang the doorbell on entering the main gate. She was prepared for many annoyances, not hatred from her mother. Ready to be answerable to Nayantara. And not put across a word of defence on her behalf. Accept her erroneous doings and hurting the sentiments of her mother's empathetic employer. She was ready for everything.

As I was wrapping up my Indian lost love story in trinkets of my bags, it was an unnerving and disrupting emotion to go through. I couldn't talk about it to anyone, or rather I wasn't comfortable talking about it to anyone. It was the end, and I knew it. After this, life would never be the same. I would never be the same again. Bangalore would never be the same. Yes, I was low and very poignant about moving out of ties of love and attachment. Much has been explained about how difficult attachment can be, yet emotional people always tend to get drawn towards it. I looked at my two-bedroom apartment and how quickly I am leaving it behind me. My roomies who were so fabulous and friendly throughout had never pricked me by digging my past with Jonathon. I felt emotionally loaded.

Before I headed to the airport, I had an unfinished business to take care off!

From a distance, I watched my house of fantasy. Didn't want to disturb the afternoon nap of two of the sweetest old couples. I might not meet them again. This house might be taken over by buildings, owing to the demand for the land. So, this was the final adieu to the dreamy Portuguese styled house where some of my syrupiest days have gone by. A tear of failure rolled down, and the next minute, I was also relieved of my choice to move out.

Putting the past behind me, I moved to the airport to my hometown Puri, where final preparations of my foreign journey would begin.

22

SCATHED BY PAST

Mrs Patrick undoubtedly was joyous to find her daughter at the door, although on face, she resented her presence. The look was grim and her past inescapably wrong. Nicola by all means looked apologetic and fragile. But Mrs Patrick was of the belief that it was just one of her theatrics. However, she asked Nicola not to step inside of Nayantara's abode of peace and to retreat from where she had been. She begged to meet her son and was remorseful of the events she was involved in. Gustavia was strict, but not heartless!

'I shall allow you to meet Adrian. And you can stay at my residence with him. I will never permit you at Nayan's residence again…not until she has forgiven you. You have no right to stay here and likewise, you had no right to sleep with her man too!'

'Mum…thank you for letting me stay in your place. I understand your wrath and won't force me on you this time. I am glad that you are allowing Adrian with me. But I would like to meet Nayantara…would like to confess and own it up. Please let me see her.'

'She's not back yet. Still in India. She won't return soon. She has extended her stay. So, your sob plan goes wasted here,' said Mrs Patrick curtly.

'I don't have one, Mum. I just wanted to apologize and also thank her!'

'Thank her?'

'Yes, her poems are an inspiration to my life, new, fresh and atypical!'

Without much ado, Mrs Patrick passed on the apartment keys and said that she'll drop by to check on Adrian. Adrian was now a sixteen-month-old gentleman. He winked when somebody laughed and grinned when anybody shouted. His anime at such a young age was too fantastic to be true. It was his latest development that Nicola had missed within these couple of months. He put his palms together when he heard a dog bark and seemed immensely joyful. He kept stretching his limbs, rolling from right to left, trying to skid off the small cot at Mrs Patricks'. His antique was seamlessly watchable. He proved to be an energetic toddler. He kept mumbling at the radio station's news, blabbering when the television was switched on. He feared none! He resented none! He knew none! He was on his own. Discovering the vastness of this planet. Yet to learn the tricks of manhood, yet to be taught the society's way…yet to fall in love and yet to gather pieces of his heart!

Nicola's unwavering thoughts paused at Adrian going through a heartbreak. Being a mother, she felt miserable only by thinking about the future which was not concrete, which was uncertain. She kissed him on the forehead and took him with her. Weeping kept her busy for the next one hour. While Adrian was playful like his dad, he had no qualities of his mother to be discussed to this day. She waited for him to fall asleep and then unpack her minimal belongings.

'O dear! I almost forgot to give this to my mother. But that also leaves me with a question on whether she would accept it or not. And these poetry books, I shall hand it to Nayantara. After all, she's a poet yet to be discovered, yet to be placed in the shelves of libraries, bookstores, and personal bookshelves! Must I meet her in the coming days, I should congratulate her on writing remarkable poems,' Nicola murmured to herself and sighed deeply that she wasn't able to meet Nayantara.

Gustavia's apartment was not as small as Nicola's. It was a nice neighbourhood condo with a fireplace, a living hall where various antiques and books on mountaineering were placed. Pictures of Gustav and Gustavia romancing in the snow-capped mountains of Alps, when they got married in a hurry wearing a heavy Eskimo jacket, a Sherpa hat at the Ski and Mountaineering church, where the wedding priest was none another one of their local acquaintances. It was crazily snowing, there was also a danger of avalanche but the two love insinuated humans-Gustav and Gustavia took their wedding vows! It was a sweet memory. Nicola again got caught in the pictures. Adrian was not much of her. She tried matching her features in the pictures to that of him. She scoffed and sighed.

'His eyes are blue, hair is brunette, he seems to have a broad jawline, thinner eyebrows, just like his dad! Will he possess any of my bad traits? O Lord, never it should be! He should be like his dad, sensitive and sensible, ethical and strong.'

In the meantime, she rested on the cot and as she was observing the thin rays of the day dimming, she fell asleep until a knock on the door woke her up.

'Scott!!! What are you doing up here?' she was shaken and agitated at him for turning up uninformed.

'I came to understand what fuck is that you are trying to do?' he seemed annoyed too.

'It was a fling! A passing affair…I thought you are a grown-up and you hardly follow people and show up at their places uninvited,' she snapped back at him.

'Does that mean you're nothing but a bitch, huh!'

'Excuse me! Were you not seeing Nayantara when you immediately switched your brains to me. She went to her home country and there your manhood chases for another woman! May I say that you are a man of honour?'

'Oh! Shut up! She trusted you more than she loved me! She made you her assistant. Gave access to her writings! She'd never let me do that! And whatever you did might lead to perjury!'

I was wrong and I don't have to hear it from you! Nobody knows what you do! You tricked her! She saved you from dying. You would be dead by now. Don't you think you used her more vehemently than me!'

There was a continuous argument at the entrance door of Mrs Patrick's apartment. Nicola after regaining her composure requested Scott not to visit her again and that she would like to undo things that she was guilty of today. 'Listen, Scott, it was my fucked-up self and I am sorry for things turning this worse. My mother won't even look at me! And more than you, I owe an answer to her and Nayantara. I've failed, and I've realized it! Now, let's stop this drama of you caring about us! Goodbye! And please don't show up!'

Scott grinned and said, 'I am sorry! I screwed up too! But I am ready to talk to Nayan and your mother! They'll surely understand us. Let's not say goodbye to each other. We can become more than a farewell! You take good care! And I can get information about people...I am quite skilled that ways. I am an undercover cop! I have never told this to anybody but you. You take time for redemption. Let me do mine! See you soon!'

Nicola was perplexed at Scott's revelation. This time it wasn't her fault. She had all ties broken with Scott. While in Leicester, she didn't even reply to his moony messages or returned his calls. Shameful was her state.

Thankfully, he left, and she didn't have to make up stories to her mother. After an hour, her mom knocked at the door as she was out with the two hounds, strolling with them in the evening. The weather suddenly turned dark with clouds engulfing the faint light, and Gustavia had to rush to her place to save them from getting drenched.

'Doesn't Adrian resemble Gustav?' asked mother after a long-hauled silence.

'Yes, the brunette hair and the jawline for sure. However, the blue eyes resemble Daniel!'

'Yeah! For sure, he was a gentleman and had kind eyes. I wish him to have traces of your dad and his!' said Gustavia.

Nicola knew what her mother was hinting at, but despite playing defensive, she kept calm and just listened to her.

'Now all I want is this child to be righteous, honest, and positive in life. These are basic traits that a human should ingrain in himself. I was not lucky enough to have a child-like that. But may Jesus bestow those blessings on your son. May you be a fortunate mother than me! The only hope I have is Adrian to be a great human being. To follow his dreams passionately. And not get dissuaded by his vices, his vicious desires like his mother.'

'Mother!' she exclaimed.

'Oh! don't say that it's pricking you. You are an impulsive, self-centred, and directionless girl. I can't pile my hopes on you. You can kill it with your invisible shovel.

'I have realized that Mom…' she was interrupted by Gustavia again as her mother wouldn't trust her anymore and ignored her redemption saga.

'How's your job at Leicester?'

'It's holding me up well. Although I wish to write someday. I have been reading a lot these days. I read poems by Nayantara too!'

'Oh yes! Aren't those marvelous pieces? Sometimes, I want to adopt her as my daughter. She's everything that a daughter should be. Care, grace, upfront, passionate, and kind!'

'You hate me, right?'

'Hate? Gustavia doesn't know what that means!'

There was another long pause which was broken by Elsa's barking. 'Elsa needs supper. I should head for the house.'

'Would you not stay here for a day?'

'Is it required?'

Nicola put her head down out of melancholy and said, 'No, you carry on. Let Adrian be here, at least?' 'He's your son!' said mother and along with her hounds and vanished into her comfortable corner.

Putting behind the fragments of first love was as difficult as learning to walk. Although as a toddler, falling down was never a cause of failure but an act of learning. Scathed by my past ruptured affair with Jojo, leads me to be a lady of compulsive attributes. I had psychological issues. No matter, I slept, ate, and wore something regularly but my mind seemed scarred by the turn of events. I felt extremely no need for emoting, socializing, or writing. It was my worst phase-no love, no life! However not being able to accept this even worsened my condition! I turned into a robot. My last few weeks in my hometown was extremely disruptive, fluctuating my mood and ending up in unhealthy banter with my folks. One evening, my mother said out of desperation that she wanted me gone and that I had transformed into a being too annoying, self-indulgent, and nagging. Only a cold place like the north can survive me. She was shocked by her only daughter turning into a rock, a self-centred rock.

And then the day arrived when my mothers' wishes came out to be true to its word. I had to leave! Leave behind the sunny land of Puri, pious for Hindus, Buddhists and Jains, and all creatures touched by God! However, I was touched by God too but it seemed love had slurped that humanity out of me. I emoted for none. I was a woman devoid of her own warmth-what a pity I had turned myself into… questioning my entire creation and all for who? The coward Jonathon Rodrigues who couldn't act his gender, his creation.

'*No Return from Here*

Return will I not, till time heals my wound
Return will I not, till silver is gone from the moon

Return will I not, till the Sun has slightest of burn on my skin
Return will I not, till His praises has torn my tongue

Return will I not, till Love keeps faking promises
Return will I not, till hurting continues in this premises

Only return will I make, when I rise above the tangles and ties
Where no man is allowed in my heart to breathe desperate lies!'

23

Marriage Proposal

London had understood and misunderstood me for the first three years of my stay abroad! And even I had reciprocated with the same level of tropical insanity to the city. I had made zero friends and zero enemies. The only friendship I had developed was with the umbrella, which had become my hood and my clothing for the unpredictable downpours. The contacts back at home diminished to a certain degree. I wasn't able to keep in touch with my friends in Bangalore, only Reena, my MBA friend was passionately in touch with me since she thought I'll succumb to the whining heart after my break up with Jonathon. But to her surprise, I became like a rock to everyone…or rather pretended to be one without emotions. I didn't cry that often but was surely entwined in my past life, my history. It's easier said than done…to control emotional upheavals, to forget love failures, to get up after somebody has hurt you badly; it was so difficult to bring your emotions to a table of normalcy! I got so engulfed with just myself and the loner life that I depended on books and my flair for reading and writing poems finally flourished again! Everyday post-work, while on the train, I kept reading. It didn't strengthen me, but it surely brought a new dimension to my dull life- my passion for poems and books! These books became my friends when I wanted to talk, my lover when I wanted romance!

'Hey Nayan! There's a social gathering tomorrow evening at Ronnie's countryside farmhouse. He seemed to have invited the entire office! Will you be accompanying us? We'll start by 7 am and it's going to be a three hours' drive from Privet Square,' asked Moli very apprehensively since she knew like other socials, my answer would be a negative one! But to her surprise, I confirmed her question by saying a yes!

Something in me wanted to visit an English countryside. 'Much have I heard about this land's countryside, let me explore it. I'll be there by the Richardson Bookstore by Privet Square dot at 6:55 am. Please fetch me up.'

Moli got puzzled and just said, 'See you Nayan', and vanished from my desk.

Ronnie's hereditary was always a talking point at work. His family hailed from the baron's family in the Eastwood kingdom of Isles, when the World War I disaster ripped the whole of England, their heritage was amongst it. The remnants of which are seen around this quaint little countryside of Isles of Rockwood. He still owns the pride of a perfect Englishman; however, the family was deprived of a huge fortune since that time. And hence, Ronnie is this boastful man of the bygone era. Although it'll be wrong to call him a racist. Just boastful!

'I have always admired the tan look that most Indians wear!' said Ronnie playfully

'Yeah, sure, stay in the Eastern part of India to adorn it! What say, Mr Walksman?'

'Just Ronnie is fine,' he said with a grin. 'No offense, Nayan'

'Call me Nayantara. I bet your tongue can master that,' I grinned too.

'Huh! Let me show you the turnip farming, here if you can follow me.'

Ronnie was a smart-looking Brit with a non-conventional sharp look, the most prominent being the eyes and the height. He wasn't a hefty guy at all and rather seemed to be leaner than men of his age. Non-muscular, I would say, a joggers' figure. He seemed to be generous, or else why would he invite the entire work folks to his farmhouse. Also, the reason was still a mystery. Why did he gather these many folks from London to Rockwood village? Many at work said that he was a strange man with strange hobbies. He enjoyed playing Polo and Snooker; and watching cricket. His favourite team was Australia instead of England, strange for any Brit. He wasn't a fan of Pete Sampras and neither did he like tennis. He had never watched Wimbledon rather he watched bike sports and used to bet his money on it too! He was in a live-in relationship. A couple of years back but was caught drunk, sleeping with the neighbour's wife and in his boxers' the next morning; risking his five years of relationship. And I also heard that the incessant 'please forgive me' messages didn't melt his girl's broken heart. Ever since, he has been single, lurking for good company and showing off his heritage village, at least whatever was left of it!

Ronnie plucked a few turnips, melons, parsley, and had it arranged on a hugely built wooden plank. As the rays of the sun wavered through this tiny spot of land, all of us were asked to gather by the wooden plank, next to the rocky dome-shaped oven. He divided us into four teams and asked us to pick one from five paper chits. Guests including me were perplexed but still did as he said without perturbing his course of action.

'Mates with Turnips can choose their recipe from the common pantry allowed. Also, for the folks getting melons and mushrooms! Parsley is common for all vegetables! Hurray! Let's prepare lunch without using any dairy products. Let's go vegan this noon!'

Few applauded as they were excited by the idea of cooking by the farm and under the stroke of serene nature. Few others' faces were nothing but about desperation and 'what the fuck' types. I was caught in-between as I could hardly follow the relevance of this gathering!

Probably, Nigella Lawson had engulfed Ronnie from all angles for sure! But Nigella's style of cooking was certainly not the newly discovered fad of veganism!

Nicola's farewell to Adrian and mother was tougher than before as they all had grown beyond their respective spaces and understood that one couldn't live without the other. However, as she was at the receiving end, she had to survive properly without them, properly with no complaints, seeking any explanations, settling minimally, and living with the support of her newly discovered friends in Leicester. Though it sounded not that difficult, sailing through this piece of the sonnet was not a smooth one to pen! She, with much composure yet turbulent emotions inside, marched forward to her reality, where she had figured out a way of living and a way of breathing.

'My Love,

Iffy is just a phase, forever is my new-found craze
Unwrapping you beneath the clothes, there wasn't only flesh and curves;
But a stoic heart of gold!

Lust maybe it was in the beginning,
Timelines were never my favourites;
Neither was defining our fateful limning!

Just hold on to this unspoken truth,
Whether you and me unite or get separated;
Our reverberations will surround the fathomless sea
Our once entwined fingers, our lip-locked saga will float over the cloud-hidden peaks
Our eyes will stand in unequivocal expressions of joyfulness
For love has befallen into our arms; and pain has once more lighted its blissfulness!
My Love, iffy is just a phase as I've found forever in this maze
--Nayantara'

Nicola owed tremendous gratitude to Nayantara, in a way that it had set her world into something she could never imagine. The unpublished scattered letters of romance, as she would love to refer to turned her into a magical yet real being. She was so lost, yet found herself incredibly.

These immeasurable, infinite lyrics of passion filled her half-full life. She had always pondered about the time of writing since a poet always embarks his/her verses in a situation measurable only in a time. Strangely, these poems had no entry of date, month, year, and even with no significant sign-ins; rather it seemed to be written stealthily with no intentions of either deliberation or publishing. Nicola wondered why and for whom…as Nayantara was more of a poet than anything else. Not only was she amplified with terrific writing skills but also, she was surmounted with a lot of tragedy.

'Tragedy makes you a higher being, Nayan. I wish to pen-like you someday', sighed the young and hurtful Nicola. Every night, she would carry the stack of uncoiled papers and read them like it's her own, type it, edit it wherever necessary. She had owned these poems and could even recite a few with no reference. She had undoubtedly become slightly meticulous these days, as she understood that money was useful and only ran into one's pocket when they worked hard for it. Robbing a bank was never on her list of jobs to do, hence, she could only strive to make it better. The return from Rickmansworth had evolved her in a non-bitter way. Not because Scott wanted to be with her but because she still saw that her mother had not totally given up on her, and also that the apple of her eyes, Adrian, wouldn't want a sulking mother. She had also believed that happiness had to be in-grown and not discovered outside of her existence! She loved Scott. His thoughts were an everyday affair to her, painfully fulfilling, however, his sudden appearance had shocked her.

The love reminiscence with Scott immediately routed her to the thoughts of Nayantara, who she so highly admired, and disregarding her for the second time would be the end of her relationship with integrity. She wanted to unmarry the thoughts of Scott. 'How' was her dilemma! The scariest moments in life were not the outcomes but always the decisions-decisions to hold on to something forever. 'Oh,

Scottie! I have to love you deeper to unlove you, to let you go!'

'Maybe, you forgot that you've someone who's seeking an answer,' said Scott aloud, while she was crossing the lane and making it to her workplace. Almost collapsed to find him in Leicester, Nicola was left with a thud in her heart on the fleet of staircases of her library. 'Ever imagined this? Eh?' asked a dejected Scott. Numbness engulfed her, and she was left with no words of wisdom. She didn't get back to Scott for reasons explicable to her heart. And neither did she welcome him with open arms. It was tough not to embrace the man you love, to make him feel stranded in a place that's not his, to make him feel unwanted and ignored! Unable to utter a word to his despair, she climbed down the stairs and run away from a situation that could bring a stormy affair yet again. Memories of their passion flashed in her mind like lightning in a dark sky but she stayed stronger, to ignore her wishful heart and march ahead unlike herself.

Scott was going through a harrowing experience, unable to absorb her reciprocation to his love! As crestfallen as he was, he failed to repair his thoughts and his actions. His tall stature caught Nicola by her wrist in a manner was to be categorized under force rather than love. And for both, love was not about force…

'You don't dare do that to me, again, Scott!' she flared up

'I apologize but you wouldn't listen. Let's be transparent Nicole to ourselves, to others for once. I carry these feelings for you and trust me these are no frills. Look at me…talk please.'

'I can't be with you if that's what you came here looking for!'

'Let's stay together?'

'Not possible.'

'Ah…alright…I know what you are thinking about me…a frivolous man. Hence, the only way to prove my love to you is to ask you…'

'Stop, please. I have to go.'

'Marry me?'

'Goodbye Scott!'

Scott was quiet and twitched his brows in worry rather than anger. He didn't see this coming his way, hence he was unprepared. He was running out of questions and even words. 'What made her change her mind?' he pondered sadly. In the meantime, Nicola kept walking away from the lane and into a foggy dimension, where Scott was not welcomed. Deprived of her attention and care, he retreated to the guest house where he was putting up for a day or two.

Rejections were not well received by Scott, usually. He was not a man who would accept defeat or failure; he took them personally and got irked, pinned, and was painfully affected! That evening in the guest house it was as if, after the war scene, dejections were lying around all over in the form of cigarette buds, scotch bottles, and some pot! He drowned himself into a vague, worthless creature, seeking attention from this lonely woman, who failed to offer him importance in her life! Scott, who was known for his courage and valour, his sharp skills of identifying crimes and criminals fell short and bruised for love. Nobody had seen this side of him, not even Nayantara. But in the midst of his love prone tragedy, he recollected Nayantara's once recited poems…

> *'Maybe there's light after darkness*
> *Or maybe there's not…*
> *Maybe I live up-to a hundred*
> *Or maybe I drown in the youthful trench*
> *Maybe there's hope after dejection*
> *Or maybe there's a great fall…*
> *Maybe you and I kiss and make-up*
> *Or maybe you and I kiss each other goodbye*
> *Whichever is the circumstance, I'll face it with equal zest,*
> *With balanced affection and with an open mind…*
> *I'll not let maybe decide what may come*
> *I'll not let maybe ruin the existing left-overs*
> *I'll not let maybe discriminate*
> *I'll not let it rule over!'*

Scott had infrequently shed tears but this was the time for him to outburst his deepened and saddened emotions. He chose to cry and cry like no other. It was a heart-wrenching scene to see a stout, huge, intoxicated man, drowning himself in impurities yet trying his best to wade through it. He realized that Nayantara came to his mind just when he needed her! And that created a lot of emotional upheaval, he kept weeping like an unstoppable downpour. That night he had learnt and unlearnt life's lessons! That night he didn't decide. That night he was at his best, with himself, supporting his tears and yet patting his shoulders. He was sloshed like a man going through life, through times that we all might have faced or would face. That night he nearly felt himself and drank further till he passed out.

24

TRYST WITH NEW BEGINNINGS

Friendship is beautiful between two living beings; man and dog, man and man, man and nature, man and books, man and music, and so many others! Friendship is slightly deviated between man and woman, when the invisible line is crossed. Many fall for friendship instantly, soak it in their syrupy nature but when lust engulfs the needs, this beauty is taken for a ride, into paths too uneven, too shaky to stand upon it! Such was my plight of friendship with Ronnie.

Ronnie's farmhouse gathering was a hit amongst all my colleagues. It was hitting me on a different tangent of togetherness, but both of us were very still and quiet about the emotions meandering inside us. It was a month to the gathering when work took its full course. I and Ronnie were indulged in the affection of just and friendliness when I received a rather unusual email from him that evening.

It said, *'Most of us don't take time to think in the wear and tear of busy life, but somehow with such business too, I have been thinking about you off-late, so much that even this beer isn't helping. The thoughts are unhealthy and I must remain a sane man! I shall not bother you! Let me manage on my own.'*

Truly, the email bothered me but wading the awkwardness, I gave a very neutral reply since I was happy in my own company, after the debacle with Jojo!

'Ronnie, I hope you are alright. It's surprising but let me know if you need to talk- Nayantara'

There were no further emails but we often met at work, passed warm gestures of being co-workers. Back of my mind, I was still surprised to see a man that was rigid and reserved, a true Brit, developing some feelings for an Asian, a brown one. He was a proud Englishman and him brewing these feelings were just out of my understanding. I took it a little sportively and did not let the email disrupt my flow of thoughts or affect my working space.

He, too, was relaxed and composed and hardly spoke about that email again. No streak of restlessness was traced, neither in his actions nor in his expressions. Even I whipped it off like some light tropical storm. Jojo's affair left a deep cut in my heart, but after these many years, it made no sense to whine about it or weep about it. Although, it wouldn't be wrong to accept that he crossed my mind when the clouds sang and the violins played, when the flowers blossomed, and also when the birds chirped. The extremely unpredictable weather in London didn't aghast me anymore. I was used to it like I was used to its trams, the subways, the narrow yet beautifully carved streets. The antique buildings, the London eye, the river of Thames, the museums, the overtly populous art galleries, expensive stores, the many Indians, too many strangers, and my exclusive feelings. Yet two months later, I received another email from him!

'Hi,

Yes, it's me again! I was just remembering you at the Rockwood! You looked great!

I think I am getting swayed by the Asian skin and the way you carry yourself. It's very classy. The entire you is too elegant. I wish we could catch up soon, yeah! Let me know. You've my telephone number, don't you? If no, mentioning it at the bottom of the email.

Ronnie'

Truly, it didn't surprise me, as I could feel that something was brewing in his heart. He seemed very observant and expressive in these emails but he didn't speak at work, which was weird! Not knowing what to reply, I turned off my computer and wanted to feel the air outside. And only then, it had started pouring badly. The unpredictable weather in London! I hope my singlehood isn't chaptered with anyone, especially at work. I was quite contented with the way things were working out. My leisure period with a handful of work friends, a few at the art gallery and Oldman theatre was just and fair to spend the rest of my life. Agreeing that my work friends and the artistic ones were very dissimilar in all ways but I was comfortable and very much myself with them. I spoke my mind, didn't speak most of the times but we connected during silence, and very well during laughter. I mostly met my art friends at galleries and workshops, we chilled with a bottle of beer (thanks to the odd cold weather where I'd started drinking often) and chips, wherein, I mostly hang out with my work friends at a coffee shop or a pub. Both were diversified but united me in a cherishing way. Probably, for this reason, I never dated during my days in London. I was bereft from the fact of getting romantic; from fantasizing men, old or young, good or great, and I was thankful for not getting into that romantic mess yet again. I was fine and was doing fine in life. Especially after opening up post spending five long years, working with the same bank, and thankfully having friends around. The relationship I had to mend was with my folks back at Puri. These telephonic conversations were fruitless and misleading. I wished that someday I would be this warm daughter if not great. And I knew that I had to work myself towards that; express my feelings and better my actions!

My aspiration in writing grew stronger and was well supported by my group in the Oldman theatre. One of my buddies, who was a playwright, had encouraged me to work on a story of my choice that he would work on and project it in the theatre. It was a huge opportunity but I could hardly come to terms with his demands since I wanted to write a marvellous piece. Putting myself under too much pressure didn't help my writing, neither was overthinking…like hell,

I was overthinking! Somebody from the art gallery suggested that I try writing with a scotch by the side. Her name was Rubail Gabbai, and her family hailed from Israel. She was one of the most abnormally beautiful people that I had come across during my days in London. I knew her for the past 3 years and we met by chance, in a funny way rather! In August 2005, when the wind had turned hasty, and I was returning from work, suddenly the tramways stopped because of bad weather which wasn't uncommon in London, everybody was asked to take the underground train. All the commuters were rushing to the nearby station, when I found a lady with a bow on her head, like Minnie mouse's, playing violin strangely, pausing in between and as she had kept a stone mould next to her, carving it into some shape… she was so high with energy that the transition was quite effortless and passers-by like me watching her, found it absolutely unnecessary yet amusing!

I walked past as the wind was engulfing the city pretty badly, however; humanity asked me to retreat my steps to the lady and ask her if she would consider winding up.

She looked at me and said, 'You too join, mate!' and giggled. The weather grew turbulent, and it was difficult for me to stand next to the pavement, under the lamp-post, as I could not restrain it. Hence, I took shelter in the nearby bookstore, named, 'Life in Second-hand'. Creatively, the book owner was a very old man with round spectacles, wrinkles forming most of his expressions, and his worn-out yet working hands arranging the old books per some order with some colourful tags. He wore a golf cap, a slightly outdated muffler, a picot overcoat hanging carelessly on the stand. The dark green sweater was ruffled at the edges, and he tried to adjust the oversized trousers that, probably with his age, were a size bigger. He seemed to me to be a classic character from a Children's English novel called Harry Potter and the Philosopher's stone, which I had started reading recently through recommendation by my friend's son-Mister Ollivander with a spectacle; I was lost in my fixation when Rubail got inside the door, all drenched and dishevelled but with a great smile.

She took off her coat and put more carelessly over the old man's coat, when he yelled at her, 'Don't dare it again, Miss!' Rubail put the coat carefully, next to the windowpane and went to the small coffee table, where freshly brewed coffee awaited her. I was, as if, just a narrator of this entire silent movie. The old man finished his work and very slowly walked towards the coffee table, pulled the wooden chair, and sat with a relieved sigh!

Rubail gestured to me to sit next to them and said, 'We'll not bite you eh! Drink some or else you'll die in this weather! Forget about reaching home tonight! Let's work on something interesting, will you?' I returned a smile since I had no other option and the company seemed warm in this dark evening of nothing. I introduced myself and they found my name so beautiful that they asked me to reiterate it! The old man was Rubail's grandfather, Mr Gabbai, who was once a playwright and an actor in the Oldman theatre. He quit acting and took over the second-hand bookstore after his father's demise post WWI; when Britain was going through a lot of socio-political and economic crisis. 'That was a difficult time, a clock in history that I wouldn't want to return or memorize!'

He still directs and writes a few of the plays at Oldman's and wishes to do the same till he falls perpetually asleep. Today's coffee was all about penning a song in a play named, 'In the evening of Nothing.' And Rubail was trying a musical chord of sadness outside the lane and was trying to create some music for the song.

Rubail, was not a conventional Israeli beauty, but a Bohemian by heart and also by looks! She liked her looks to be unmatched, since she believed matching attire with accessory and the heart with the mind was utterly boring and bland. 'One should only match a smile to a face,' is what she regularly used to say. She had expressive, rounded eyes, which was the mirror of her heart. It was so kind and beautiful. Although she used to continually blame her late father for the pug-like nose, however, she seemed to enjoy the small of it sitting on her face. A genetic memory of her father, who she mentioned on almost all the occasions we've met. Another most striking feature about Rubail was her warm personality, and those positive vibrations that she carried, which made a stranger like me feel at home. She carried some healing essence, some serenity that many found divine!

So, returning back to that evening of where Mr Gabbai had inspired me to pen my poem…with terrible weather outside but a passionate one inside. A slight smile with a sigh had crossed my face when I heard two unknown geniuses working on it…

'In this evening of Nothing, when I stumbled on my shadow abruptly,
I discovered that I am more Humane than you!

Hey you Nightfall, I assumed you to be dark and deadly,
But darker is the shade of an unknown you

The End wasn't despiteful,
It was the cold in you which was this distasteful,
And hence, I regarded my Silence more conveying than your malice

The Nothing has nothing to snatch away from me…it only makes me ponder,
And in this evening where Nothing has so much to offer…
I chose it over your hollow show…
I chose Nothing over your shallows

In this evening of Nothing, when I was emancipated…
I found Love all around me than in you'

Since that lyrical evening, Rubail and Mr Gabbai were closer to my heart, inspiring me to write again, after the tragedy of wrecked love, and explained to me that the most appropriate way of releasing your anguish, emotions is through music and writings! The believer in me started penning, and I felt at ease with my life, with no complaints but a lot of relief. An inspiring set of friends can do wonders to your non-aspiring life. And so, did it happen! Finally, the wild world of the west was embracing me into its cold arms, gifting me friends from all spheres of life.

While I started working on the play and was literally trying to lay along, Ronnie's midnight email disturbed me a little.

'Either I'm turning into a chain smoker or a moronic drunkard. This loneliness of mine keeps looking for you in all ways possible. If you think I'm

being romantic, probably I'm the last pragmatic man to do that! But why don't you respond is what's making me go mad!

-Ronnie'

Blimey! Now how am I supposed to interpret this! The last email was sent on a Friday and today is just a Sunday. And I didn't think it was urgent to connect over the phone. It broke the flow of my thoughts; the writing was incomplete and dark clouds covered the beautiful snow-peaked mountains. It was a sign of a dark thunder, I could sense…

'Hi Nayan, how are you today?'

'Gosh…you…Good evening!' I said, being surprised at Ronnie's sudden office greeting.

'Would you mind talking to me for a minute?'

'Of course…not, tell me?'

'Not here.'

'You want to catch up for tea or coffee?'

'Not really. I want you to note down my cell phone number. And possibly share with me yours if any!'

'I don't mind noting down your number.'

'I got to pace up work now. See you!'

His thoughts and actions were so different. He behaved just so normal at work. Like he carried no feelings. His emails were equally filled with troubled emotions, confusions, and a certain degree of likeness. I spent the next hour toggling my brain to 'how could that be' and post that I returned to work. Thinking about Ronnie was kind of exhausting to me, hence I focused to change directions. This trial of confusion was unnecessary, and hence, a mitigation plan was necessary. I chose work and writing to survive properly with a great many friends…

25

TRIALS OF CONFUSION

Nayantara's first poem titled 'Trials of Confusion', left Nicola in fragments of bereavement as she had cast away Scott in a manner that was not appropriate to her personality or her feelings. She felt for Scott, but she didn't want a life caught in mazes and complications, as she had already made a mistake by disturbing Nayantara's interest. She didn't want a miserable life. Respect and resolution were on her mind and she wanted Adrian to be a great man, learn a great many things from her. Hence, she consciously decided to take one role at this time. The role of a mother and not that of an estranged lover.

No matter how strangulated her emotional being was, no matter how much she wanted to run to Scott but she wanted to prove herself to be above this, above these confusions. She wasn't able to sleep that night till dusk, only when she saw the Sun up. She smiled with a heavy heart, knowing that love was not meant for her, and being a romantic wouldn't help. The thoughts of how Nayantara had embraced her persona at Rickmansworth consoled her, how she had felt confident in handling her personal stuff, puffed her up so much that she was now a fan of Nayantara's work. And got inspired by it.

Waiting for Nayantara to return to Rickmansworth from India

instilled a lot of patience in her and in return, this brought her some peace. In the whirlpool of disturbance, she was waiting for her turn, to be pardoned for something done in the haste of romance. She often quoted Nayantara's poems at work and was many times admired by the library members. The suggestions offered were to publish her work as soon as possible. To approach an agent of repute and who could help to pitch with literary publishing houses. She required Nayantara's permission; her return.

My folks' oddity with technology didn't surprise me as we sat in the super posh airport lounge of Mumbai. They didn't bother about unknown stuff. Neither did they care that they were in a lounge where many celebs parked themselves for exclusion. They carried a face that didn't question or judge, but observed. And that made me ponder what maturity does to us, what being old actually denotes- not brittle bones, wrinkled skin, medical ailments but life's experiences, its cycle, its observations. Watching them over was a pleasure, noticing their calmness was peaceful. It was their second international flight after many years, and it did not affect them, no anxiety, no travel stress, no opulence, no show-off! I'd never seen my folks this serene. I enjoyed it and drew a lot of optimism. It was peaceful to observe.

We were travelling business class hence the long journey would be less hectic. There was enough leg space for them to stretch, be comfortable. The food served was Indian, and they liked it. My mother was more experimental in trying out drinks than my father, who was frowning at the fact that my mother was trying out alcohol. My mother nudged me and seemed to be playful and giggled at my father, 'Look at him, judging me! Who has stopped him to try it?'

My father and I had a very conservative relationship! We were certainly not friends; hence, I couldn't suggest that he try a drink, and neither could I take one. In the interest of no-nonsense in the flight, I refrained from drinking.

'Bapa, would you mind a soft drink?'

'Not required! I am fine. I am shocked at your mothers' audacity to drink. Please let me be,' he said and pulled a magazine forcefully from the seat pouch, denoting that he didn't appreciate the gesture of my mother suddenly evolving, even when we didn't land in the west.

'Western influences have ruined our culture,' stated he with angst. By this time, my mother was a beer down and was a little tipsy as it was her first. She started blabbering about her life as a new bride.

'Buli…do you know how miserable my life was as a new bride? Eh? You were not born and if you had been, I would have been socially outcast by everybody who raised me in a conservative family. I was born in a quaint little village called Narendrapur, 30 kms away from Puri. It had no electricity distribution, so lanterns and lamps were my guiding light. Being the brightest student in my family, my grandfather wanted me to complete school and take up a profession of an educationist, as he believed, women could do wonderful in the art of educating people. However, he was the only progressive-thinking man that I know till date! The family was fulfilling to him; however, he didn't want to have four sons and three daughters! None of his daughters were serious about education, more so because of the scavenging relatives, who wanted daughters of the family to marry off and sail for another life. My grandmother was patriarchal and her views had always alarmed my grandfather! I faintly remember them arguing. However, my grandmother always had her way out. As I was the second granddaughter of marriageable age, she insisted me on getting married at the tender age of 17! I had revolted with my parents but in vain. They had no say as my father was not a great contributor to the family's wellbeing. I was married off, couldn't stand to protest for my life's decision, couldn't stand for getting educated that I was so good at! Mostly, I was a meagre human being, a fearful one! I was sent off to Bhubaneswar, as your father had a job in Bhubaneswar. I used to only write to my grandfather and nobody else. He used to reply to me in equal zest. Post two years of my settlement, the letters stopped, and I was worried. Then came news not too pleasing to my ears of him passing away! Although, he wrote a small note of life's misgivings for me to remember him forever!'

I was surprised at this side of my mother as I thought her to be patriarchal too. But it is wonderful, what alcohol can do to us! I tried calming my mother's sad experience and asked her to share the letter that my great grandfather had addressed to her!

She continued, 'Yes! I will share the letter with you. He had titled it, 'Trials of Confusion,' she said smiling slightly. As she was hoping me to be a quiet listener to her never mentioned life.

'Your father's family was extremely orthodox about me reading novels by great Odia authors, as they thought, it'll erupt rebellious feelings and instil unwanted romances in me. I, being the harbinger of taking the family legacy forward, must be decent from all the spheres of society. My father-in-law threw away my books. Also, it was supported by other members of the family. It broke me down to depression. I'd treasured those books! They were my friends, my liberation! Your father did not interfere, and neither did he stand up for me, as a husband. My mother-in-law was a diseased woman and spent mostly in bed. Although she had kind eyes, she couldn't do much about my situation. I was fearful to voice out my anguish. Thoughts wandered, insecurity purred, and I indulged myself in being a docile animal- a voiceless daughter-in-law, a spineless wife, focusing myself on household chores! And when few winters passed by, I was taunted for not bearing a child, for being the talk of the town, not being able to reproduce, which a woman must in-order to prove her worth in the family. After my grandfather's death, as if, I was orphaned and there was no support from my family too,' as she spoke, she turned warm with emotions. But still continued, 'You were born after ten years of my marriage, your father was relieved, I was calmed to see you cuddle besides me, as I thought I finally will find a friend in you. My father-in-law and other members were furious. He literally disowned you since you were a girl, a mere nothing to his legacy, his family!'

'Thankfully, your father was a little compassionate and clever, and moved out of Bhubaneswar, to Puri, stating that he had better prospects of work. My father-in-law somehow understood that I have influenced my husband and addressed me as an evil-intent female.

He was infused with anger and jealousy, also power and insanity. He literally asked your father to leave and to vanish forever. Your father was referred to as a crooked son and a terrible person. Although he never admits it, I know that he is hurt deep inside. You know Buli, only people close to you can dagger you that bad, and the wounds never heal, it just gets buried but not healed!' as she spoke, my father seemed to be a quiet listener too!

I suggested my mother have something as she was talking her heart out for a long time now. She excused herself to the restroom and my father looked a little assured that she was fine now. He had never witnessed an emotional outbreak of hers, and neither did I ever have such an intriguing memory with her! I was remorseful at her condition but consoled that she had been through it and that now it's over! There was no more of it. There was no 'Trial of Confusion', nobody as vindictive and nasty as her father-in-law.

This took me back to my poem which had a similar tone of words and it was too titled the same. Mostly, I had written it in one of my pocketbooks, which was meant to note down postal addresses and telephone numbers. After only meeting the magical duo, Mr Gabbai and Rubail were inspired to take up writing seriously. It took me back to almost a decade when in that same old weary second-hand bookstore, I had a phase going on and Mr Gabbai had suggested I pour it out to feel better. Post Jojo's episode in Bangalore, I'd lost interest in writing but thanks to London, and these two-special people, who saved me from drowning again!

'Trials of Confusion

Never they who love will be the ones who prick
Never they who nurture, must be the ones to trick
Never they who are around should be the ones to disappear
For Trials of Confusion must never engulf, must never be
For life has known only a few aspects
For life has always allowed us to introspect
To touch the skies and even beyond
To flip the earth and also to its respond

To fly and also to fall
To rise and also to halt
To sprint and get injured
To love, like, and embrace ambience from all spheres
For Trials of Confusion must never be, must never be!
--Nayantara'

26

THE AWKWARD PHASE

'Through my body, you've entered my soul,
O my beloved, cast me not into a limited role

For I am henceforth, Liberated….
With your love, charmed and also appreciated!

The rhyming minds and the swift beating of our hearts
You seemed nervous, yet honest with no harm

The symphony at which we both saw light
The stance where we both discovered our sights

'Fallen in love' wouldn't be an overstatement
As Twinning minds never fail divine engagement

Accepting that my dream is very far-fetched,
Alas! Dream is the only place where I see us etched…'

I showed this piece of my nervous writing to Rubail, at her art gallery. The person she was assured me, she'll burst out laughing and teasing me for the rest of the evening. But I wanted to brave it all and take a second opinion.

'Puny writing, is it?'

'Gosh! Nayan! Allow me please,' she got up from the stool and bowed in a grand way, as if I was the greatest poetess of all times. 'Now I am so sure that you'll end up writing a great story someday, and I would enact it! How's that?'

'C'mon Ruby, that's too ambitious for a feeble, mundane person like me! I earn my bucks and have travelled over 6000 kms away from my hometown, that was a striving journey! Putting up a decent life in a place so far is my achievement. I don't strive further; I don't look beyond. I am fine. Writing is not my kind of thing.' I excused myself to the coffee vending machine, placed at the corner of Ruby's work area.

Rubail was an intelligent woman that I had met and she knew exactly what to say when. She had a sense of right time-right place ingrained meticulously. Hence, she spoke nothing and let me be.

'How's your boyfriend doing?'

'I don't have any…not now!'

'C'mon! That guy in your office, that arrogant Brit, you talked about, his farmhouse gathering, his strange email timings, and even stranger content…all of that?'

'As you mentioned, strange is the king here!'

'Yeah and are you not into his strangeness? It seems you've liked his oddity. I can read it, baby!'

I preferred to keep quiet and let silence do the talking. Definitely, she didn't know a thing about my writing, the way I used to pen down for Jojo, our sweet affair, back in the days of history…digging by the grave is not what I wanted here, hence, nobody in London knew about my past affair, the reason was quite simple, it was past and it was odd!

After months of squabbling about the cold war with Ronnie, finally, I agreed to meet him to talk about his confusing and hypocritical state of mind- his so-called discreet emails and his personality crisis.

The office hours dealt by him were just those iffy greetings, cold smiles, and negative vibrations. But unlike him, his emails were full of emotions, his current life, his choices, his desires and his strong attraction towards Asian females, his authentic British legacy, his great grandfather's expedition to India during his service to the Company, his personal diaries about India, the anarchism of the cold officers, the divided Indians, the helpless Kings, the cruelty, his likeness for India and its history, it's resilience as land, it's cultural diversity, the *Bhagavad Gita* and much more! I was overloaded with his information, his life's likeness, and situations. But one thing that struck my heart was his empathy towards my land, my people! Also, the commonality of being philosophical. He had shared a lot about himself.

Post work on a Friday, where London offices shut down by 4 pm, I stayed back a little longer to get dressed up at work. There were few foreigners like me, winding up for the weekend, and I was caught up in mixed emotions. Probably, Rubail was right when she said that I am kind of attracted to his odd-self, surely not his arrogance; but I also find him quite intriguing, in some ways that even I was uncertain about.

Attraction is another terrible thing, it harms your mental state to an extent that you sometimes end up liking that person, factoring in no sensible reasons. Your tastes and interests go for a toss, you develop a streak of unconscious biases towards that person, and although you don't like his worldly dealings, his uncompassionate persona, you still are drawn… for some flaws of your own past life! These relationships, if developed, result in nothing but a delusion, pain and are inconclusive- it's nothing but a karmic affair, an affair that holds no good, no peace! And somewhere in my senses, I predicted being highly disappointed by this man as things were awry yet attractive. That's a terrible world to be adjusting to. I was so doubtful about him and the way he would want us to be. Never was I this confused, not even when I saw his first email. Or maybe I was over-thinking!

At 'London's 44' pub, I was already drunk. His message stated that we must catch up at six in the evening, however, it was already 30 minutes past the decided time. I was not furious since I hardly had any expectations. The ambience of the pub was relaxing, only buzzing with great old classics, few of them were French numbers too. There was supposed to be a band playing at seven-thirty and it was a quite popular band across this street. People were reserving their places with excitement and energy. Mostly couples, chittering their heart out as if this was their only moment, their only space where memories could be made. I was feeling a little relieved since there was no need for me to create any memories. I was quite content that way. How my decisions, whether right or wrong led me here, where I found not only work but great friends. And if I compare greatness with minor disappointments, it seemed to be the right balance. The only thing I should care about or rather start mending is my relationship with my folks, back in India. Probably, I must call them over to London!

'Hey, do you want to repeat?' perturbing my thoughts was the attendant. 'Yes, please.' I said in a neutral tone though I was a little irked. With no prying eyes of the past, I sat well, enjoying my singlehood moments, not pondering about my past but the moment that I was in.

'Please excuse me, Nayan! I was stuck!'

I turned back to the familiar voice that I have so less conversed with! 'Who said I was waiting for you? Rather I was quietly enjoying my minutes here! It's a great place to be at...especially on a Friday evening.'

'That's bloody great!' Ronnie smiled conservatively and was kind of checking me out, which strangely I enjoyed! 'You may compliment me, word it out!'

This time he blushed heartily and said, 'You've always made me high! Just you around me and I am woozy! It was very tough to keep these brewing emotions of likeness inside of me,' as he spoke these stupendously with the right blend of romance and honesty, I was impressed, knowing very well that this affair of oddity will ruin me emotionally. I could foresee it but allowed him to talk his heart out.

We both were a couple of drinks down and suddenly I wanted to change the glass of my cocktail as it was getting a little awkward to drink, Ronnie stopped talking and started gazing at my antics very attentively.

When I was done whining about the glass to the attendant, my eyes caught his, and we were kind of in a moment, which was infusing desires of want and needs! He was not a romantically inclined guy, he was too blunt, on the face and he didn't care how the other person might take things. However, tonight, he seemed a little polite yet selfish towards his feelings for me he claimed to carry over the time.

'You are my first ever workplace-mess. The minute I had set my eyes on you, I was on an abnormal extremity; considering the fact that I had just, back then, broken up with my partner! It was awful to be attracted to someone, who you have nothing in common with! Look at you, so full of energy, so vibrant, with such a pretty face, full of light! And I am such an introvert about my own insidious feelings! I am opening up after eight months of us meeting, I couldn't even speak to you at my farmhouse gathering. What a miserable soul I must be!'

I had befallen by his confessions. Nobody would've gathered an iota of his ideas about me. I was quieter than ever! Just trying to understand him. The alcohol was doing its wonders, and I gradually liked him sitting in front of me and talking whatever shit he could present me with!

He continued after requesting me to change the seats from indoors to outdoors.

'I used to not care how I looked earlier but trust me now after so many months, today, I tried to look good, at least put an effort to look nice! Do I look okay to you? Huh? What's the matter, you are never this silent?'

Whilst I was trying to understand what this meeting was all about and listening to him carefully, I suddenly drooled my cocktail and was clumsily trying to wipe it off when he commented, 'You look extremely cute being clumsy! But I am wondering what turned you into this silent audience today!' My eyes kind of popped out with his 'cute' remark and I felt so uncomfortably happy! He kept on with his saga, but this time he talked about my oddly long and skinny fingers and that it's strangely attractive! Moronically, I placed my hands on his; he tried to cup my hands by placing his drink aside and began looking into my eyes with kindness. I was swept off with the alcohol acting like a love potion. To confess the truth, I enjoyed whatever silly thing happened that evening. Didn't utter, 'stop it' 'shush' to him. We kept gazing at each other and I kept on blushing. When I was a little sober, I tried to act a little sane and ask, 'So, Ronnie, what do you want from me? I am confused and my emotions need a track to walk on, now it's going haywire!'

Ronnie took off his hands from mine and started drinking again!

'Nayan, you are not the first woman who's sitting with me on an evening of such kind. Let me be very honest with you. I have had quite a chunk of women in my life, beginning from grade 9, yeah, right from elementary school,' he paused and took his glass to gulp some more and continued, 'so, I am not new to the nuances of women, their needs, their disturbances, their interferences, their desires, their romances! I'll assume to know it all! You'll be my 13th who I have had a huge crush on ever since I saw you. I know we have conflicting personalities. But if you expect some kind of romanticism from me, probably this won't end up well! I am not a romantic and I don't like calling names, just to make sure you don't start with that woozy stuff. I find it stupid. My last partner was very cooperative on these terms and if you want to be with me, my expectations must be set right.'

I looked at him with utmost confusion and horror. He kept tale-telling about his preferences. I was drunk, and I wanted to ask him again, 'So, you want me to be whatever you like, not what I am like… huh?'

'Absolutely not! I want nothing from you! I want us to be friends!' he said smilingly.

'Oh really! Probably this is a trending concept of the west now, you refer to romantic relationships as friendship, to cover up your commitment phobia?' I asked shrewdly before I headed for the restroom, a little perturbed, and the drinks had gradually started receding, giving me a bite of the reality. In the restroom, as I was waiting for my turn to use the toilet, I realized that this date is turning out to be sour. Morose engulfed me and I started feeling bad for how this was ramifying into. I was surprised to relate to my emotions since I had expected little from this meeting earlier but couldn't confirm my expectations now. My notions about this date and the feelings I'd gathered through it were very varied. I think Rubail was somewhere correct in saying that I had begun liking him!

On returning to the terrace, most seats were emptied and couples or friends or whatever these guys referred to, had let their hair loose! It was only Ronnie to be checking outside the terrace, looking at the lanes which had dimmed to darkness but he still held a glass, half full. This time, it looked like a gin! And he was still himself, upright, and not at all moony!

'Hey! I'd put in a lot of efforts in my previous relationship, I loved her, and I still do. I had beaten the shit out of realism to be with her, and it was a promise! It didn't last…the relationship. But I carry feelings for her. You've to get used to that. I won't or even try to stop being myself. I am being very honest with you! If you are thinking of a relationship with me, forget it, it'll not work. I see a lot of expectations in you and you've been quiet ever since we met, which is highly unlikely. Short-term friendship is what I am looking forward to. Nobody questions anyone when they exit. No explanations, no limitations, no jealousy, no commitment! But you seem to have a problem, your questioning face, huh?'

'You mean friends with benefits, no strings attached, not involved emotionally, yet involved physically, right?' I said with utmost disgust.

'Nayan, I am sorry, this date was a bad idea, I can't afford to get emotionally invested.'

'Probably, I should get going, anyway it's getting late.'

'Why not!' he stated, 'May I help you with the cab?'

'Not really. I'll take the underground or the tram if it's up and running. Thanks for offering help.'

'No problem at all! I am done for the evening too, let's leave together,' he said as if nothing major had happened, nothing of relevance was discussed.

I was silent, and we walked past this happening pub of London's 44, which created an indelible scar in my heart. I was flushed and felt saddened by how events had turned out to be! Strangely; I was the one to avoid, and it was me who seemed to be entirely affected by the fall of it! He accompanied me to the underground, our eyes kept meeting, and he kept asking me to voice it out. I was quiet and remorseful. The train entered the station, and we turned our heads towards each other. I looked at him and he pursed his lips. We tried to embrace but failed… he tried smiling to let it go.

I smiled too, and the saga of oddity between the two most unlikely people began!

27

NICOLA'S TRIUMPH

Nicola, dearly addressed a letter to Scott, which she intended to post it at the address once given by him. He usually stayed in London since his main department of work was located there. Often, he travelled for that was his job. She was quite certain about the letter reaching him on time and in good of his health. She never meant to deceive him as she was a 'transformed soul' now and reading had done something wonderful to her imprudence, so much that she got wary of her true worth, her responsibilities and also learnt a lot about being in love, to be kind to most and perform duty as that defines us!

Mostly on Fridays, post her library duties, she returned to Bella and her small tea discussions. She had tasted a variety of tea with her, as Bella was a tea enthusiast. Her taste buds liked earl grey the most. That evening too, she headed to Bella's shop, which was usually a major attraction, mostly for the middle-aged men and women. And she, as a shop-owner, was quite an enterprising lady.

She would on days narrate her encounter with sexually depressed customers, some other days about hyper old aged women who want to try all the toys. Also, about this customer, Veronica Jones, who was a regular customer and was quite famous for her adult parties at her secret mansion somewhere. 'Not only was she filthy rich, but she was wise too! Just that she was unfortunate in love!' would sigh Bella. 'Sometimes, I wish to close this shop and work at an old age home or rehab centre to help the needful. Share love, care for the ones needing it,' as she said, she sipped the tea and then sighed again.

'Why don't you work at an old age home or sobriety centre,' she asked Nicola who was in some thought of hers. 'Ahh…sorry, just missed that part, please come again?'

'You are so engrossed today, my dear! I wish well for you. But is everything okay? I mean to ask about your son?'

'Oh yes! He's doing good. Mother is taking very good care of him,' and she smiled slightly while trying to focus on her thoughts and then the tea.

'Then who is it about? If I may ask?'

She sighed out of slight exasperation and still kept on with the tea. 'I have somebody's manuscript; a work of poetry and I want to get it printed as in published. She's a new poet but she's very inspiring. Would you know anybody?'

'Publisher, you mean? But that isn't your work, right?'

'I want to surprise her, indemnify for my incorrect conduct in her life. You can say that if I present her with this surprise, probably I'll be redeemed, feel lighter, peaceful, and if possible joyful. She's been a great support throughout. It helped me change the course of my life. My perspective broadened, so much that I understood some aspect of life and love!'

'Ah, Nicole! It's so deep! Even if I don't know anybody in publishing, I'll try to look out.'

'In the meantime, I'll ask in the library. But I am a little scared too, as maybe she might not like her poems being printed.'

'Oh! not to worry at all! All poets and writers of the time would wish their work to be published! It might bring her immense happiness. Your thoughts are very well-intended. You just have to drive it. But are you sure, it's only this?'

'Meaning?'

'Are you sure it's not the love bug biting you?'

Nicola grinned and craned her neck to avoid Bella's eye contact. 'It isn't! I have no time, no energy, and no love for that kind of love.' As she said she looked at her watch which was ticking away faster than she thought. She had to return to nowhere but her apartment and she was making the move, Bella insisted she stay back.

'Stay back. It's only Friday and you've nothing to do, no mundane chores. Tell me who has made you into this solemn affair? Please don't hesitate as I am nothing but a friend,' as she said she'd cupped Nicola's hands out of support and care.

Nicola looked dazed as she wasn't expecting these questions from Bella, who knew nothing about her state of heart. Just that she had witnessed a better version of her, a sorted, responsible one. The previous versions of Nicola were abrupt, fickle, and nymphic. Bella understood that her friend isn't comfortable and hence she parked her questions for some other day. Nicola wanted to answer but was reticent as she had a fear of judgment. And she had nobody to probe her wellbeing, nobody to ask her questions, nobody to look out for her…although these things made her sad, but she rather kept it under her purview. When Bella probed, she was very surprised and wanted to blurt out the truth and she wanted to confess that it was tougher to be without her son, her mother and that she has a great likeness for Scott, also that Scott was Nayantara's romantic interest but they didn't have any commitment, anything relevant, and that Scott had proposed her for marriage but she wasn't ready as she for once wanted to prove her worth to herself. She had shooed away Scott since she couldn't take the responsibility of another man's love at this point. And also, that she wanted to confess everything to Nayantara and feel guilt-free about her unspoken relationship with Scott. And that her poems had inspired her to till this day, to live, to breathe and to enjoy singlehood, to enjoy imagination, to enjoy romanticism, to enjoy nature, to live by her own…

She sighed while she was waiting for Bella to close her shop and take her out for a small gathering planned at Bella's place. Later, while detouring away from Bella's place, she was told, 'It's a secret party, very discreet it's supposed to be, hence shush!' Nicola smirked and asked, 'Are you up to some kind of naughtiness?' Bella immediately laughed heartily and said, 'In this age, isn't that the only choice one must make, huh?' They both laughed to their heart's content and headed towards Veronica Jones' gathering. Nicola's presumptions were intimidating her as she had heard about Veronica being filthy rich and usually hosting host parties at her someplace else mansion!

They crossed the Leicester square, the Mid-way junction of the great market of Hobstone, where people were bustling with the flea shops and food junkies were hogging onto the evening supper. It was turning cloudy and greyish; the sky in England changed more colours than its people, than its stiffy trees! Once Hobstone was left behind, they arrived at a crossroad of alleys, peculiar ones rather. Each leading to some strange land that Nicola had ever forayed into, explored. Bella held Nicola's hands firmly and directed her to be as grave as ever. She took the alley to her right and stopped at the old book depot named, 'For those stories…that don't end'! The place seemed haunted and was extremely creepy during dawn. They waited for something to happen, probably, and then found a man with two women waving at them. Bella waved at them back. Finding the entire evening strange, Nicola wanted to flee. She felt so bumpy that evening and to add to her awkwardness, Bella's husband was nowhere to be found.

Bella kissed the man and the other two women were onlookers and had nothing but a straight face. All the more petrified, she wanted to leave immediately, but they kept on walking to yet another strange, dark, and dingy alley. 'Bella, I'm scared! I want to retreat, please, let's go!' Bella shushed Nicola, and said, 'Not to worry, I am there with you. Things will be fine. It's your first time, hence, you are scared! Trust me.' 'And not every dark thing, every dark lane must end in darkness. Light shows up, look at it, towards the extreme right?' Nicola twisted her neck hesitantly and discovered a small beam of blinking colourful lights from nowhere and sighed out of relief. She followed Bella and ignored the rest of them.

'Not every dark lane must end in darkness,' she kept mumbling to herself repeatedly till they reached the lighted spot full of hues of happiness. It was a garden of some sort with fencing around it, never to be seen in a place that she'd spent most of her life. Although she wasn't an ardent traveller, however, she'd known most places in Leicester. The light in the tunnel was dazzling, and as if from the forbidden woods, she could see the light. She smiled with relief and looked at Bella. 'You were unnecessarily scared, weren't you?' 'Yes! I was.'

Out of the other three companions, the gentleman who'd kissed Bella, finally smirked at Nicola's childishness and asked, 'Only when there's darkness can there be light! Only when you find shadows must you find reflections!' he smirked again and introduced himself as Mr Cunningham. He was tall and charming, but his features yelled to be too Scottish, and with that heavy accent, he impacted Nicola. Bella saw Mr Cunningham trying to strike a conversation with Nicola. She smiled at it and excused herself from the scene with the other two women.

It was titled, 'The Dusk Party-Embracing the Black'. Nicola was uninformed about the theme and any details, as she was uninvited to the party. The host was none other than the rich lady, Ms Jones, and the party embankment was one of her many spots that she owned in the English land. Figuratively she was an attractive woman with an impeccable blend of grace and poise. Nicola was hugely drawn to her vibrancy and joyousness. She wanted to pose with her for pictures but restrained, thinking it to be too silly of her. She got herself into a cosy cane-wood chair along with a bottle of beer. Allowing her senses to feel relaxed and the evening to absorb into her, she started looking at the set-up of colourful lights suspended from the branches of small trees, the jazz band, and the consciously fluttering people. It felt warm in this cold weather. On observing the entire vicinity, she found it to be too colossal to be true. However, she discovered many who were engrossed in their world and seldom cared about the others, some were drinking all by themselves, few were liaising and laughing to their heart's content and a handful of others were like her, reserving their physical self to a corner and watching over. There she spotted a small house at one corner, however, with a mammoth garden, many water fountains with hues too magical. 'Maybe two hundred people or maybe three hundred...,' she murmured as Bella was busy with a handful herself.

'The guest list was 275 until few guests bought guests of their own,' said Mr Cunningham in a soft voice conforming to her confusion. She was reticent enough to add further to his statement. 'So, what do you do, Miss...?'

'I...work in the Brookshire Library as an assistant,' she said hesitantly.

'Oh! that's nice.'

'I work in London. Have a family business to run. However, I have a house here. I usually stop by Veronica. She's a dear friend.'

'Nice to know. It's just that I hardly know anybody other than Bella.'

'I don't see a problem in that. We gather to know each other. And Veronica's parties are lavish yet have the human connection, hence you'll like it.'

'Hmmm... I am mesmerized by these lights. It's brilliance enlightened!'

'Yeah lady! She has a sense in all of these. Very creative in that way. And you must see her sketches and sculptures. They are supremely articulated.'

'Is she a sculptor or an artist?'

'Nobody knows yet. When I first met her, she was into painting and she owned a gallery in Versailles in France, where she used to travel often and probably, she has a house there too. A couple of meetings later, she stopped travelling to her gallery and handed it over to her Italian fiancé who is a renowned artist by himself. A few months later, she started working as an art curator at the Picasso Art Agency, quite a name in Europe! I moved out of England for work, and now I am informed that she's started a publishing firm of her own where she encourages writers and poets! Quite a hell of a job profiles she's had,' Mr Cunningham smirked at Ms Jones stretched job roles and biodata. However, his tone was full of excitement and pride while he narrated about Ms Jones. Nicola thought so and was quite interested to be introduced to Veronica now. As she watched her over, she found that under the glam fitted clothes and sparkling diamonds, there was a resilient lady who has features of a Russian princess! One of the biggest eyes that she's come across, with invariably smaller yet fuller lips, thick eyebrows or probably tattooed, and a small blunt nose which added to her beauty. Until today, Nicola took utmost pride in carrying her mother's beautiful huge eyes with luminous eyelashes, which today stood untrue. Although, petite, Veronica carried a greatly alluring personality. And with so many feathers in a cap, Nicola was undecided whether to address her talent or restlessness. But she somehow got her wishes mapped onto Veronica's current state of affairs, her publishing business.

'If you may help me with the name of her publishing firm, I'll be so glad,' she inquired to Mr Cunningham.

'Do you typically talk formally?' and he gave a good loud laugh after sipping his scotch.

'Sorry!'

'C'mon, what do I call you?'

'Nicola…my name is Nicola Patrick.'

'So, Nicole, the publishing firm is called Writers & Poets Ltd.'

Her heart was full of content as if the stars had granted her something valuable. And she now can take off the burden of deceiving Nayantara, by presenting her with one of her most valuable scriptures of inspiration, a published one! Never in recent history, she felt this triumphant, never in this life had she dedicated herself to the cause or effect of anything. Never had she stretched her arms of help to anyone… well…she had to begin from somewhere!

28

MENDING IT IN LONDON!

They made it to London after ages and I was super eager to get their acknowledgement on how and what of everything about this place has or hasn't changed, as if I owned it, as if London was my place. It wouldn't be wrong to say that I'd taken most of life's scenic moments from this place, even more that I'd got in from Goa. I matured here, withdrew from my miseries, started feeling each and every breath with calmness, and got some amazing friends, and to top it all a great financial stance. I was so confident and content with whatever I'd to deal with here, it only taught me and helped me grow further and better. I'd booked a hotel in south London, which was the hub of Indians and Pakistanis. The first time my parents had travelled so far, they'd preferred to stay with their friends at the sub-urban corner and could not visit the mainland.

'O da Connor, although was an Italian name but had everybody in it from the sub-continent,' I explained to my father. He nodded as he was a little out of place. His attributes were not matching to the people around him. However, he kept calm and proceeded quietly, with no fuss. My mother was superbly energetic and wanted to explore everything, unlike the last time. I saw her wanting to conquer the fort, jump off the cliff and go paragliding with mountaineers, cross the hollow, and overcome all possible obstacles as a different person! She was that mesmerized by this land and its ancient style. 'I don't want to go back,' is what she told me. My father was as surprised as I was! I confirmed by saying, 'Okay, I'll plan so you don't have to!' She's hardly been this ecstatic all her life, and now when she was finally seeing something outside her demarcations, she felt like a child again. We didn't stop her from anything since she was joyful.

I pondered what a new place does to the most hesitant people, introverts, reserved ones; what exploration brings in you! How beautiful are awareness and discovery, and yet there's so much to be unearthed!

We checked in to the sub-urban Tuscany styled hotel, which wasn't colossal but cosy. On inquiring from the hotel's manager, Dalbeerjeet Singh, it was found that this was as old as World War I itself, over 100 years old. Such a delectable structure could withstand the mighty cruelty of human's ego! As I smirked to myself, no sooner my folks were tired from the long journey and wanted to rest. We'd opted for two small rooms, each room next to each other and also facing the streets of south Croydon. It was fun after all this time to spend with my parents. It's truly believed and said that given time and space, few troubled relationships overcome and stand out.

'Let's meet for lunch at 12:30 pm?'

'Yes, and I also want to shop!'

'Sure, Ma!'

'I want to buy boots and a pair of trousers, may I?'

'You must, Ma! And also, an umbrella. It's a must for anybody living in London.'

My dad gave a good laugh at her subtle demands and said, 'You are exploring youth, it looks!'

'Maybe,' said my mother, and they both exchanged glances of comfort. And I could feel the comforting vibe around. Excusing myself, I checked into my room, which had a huge TV screen, a basic necessity for most people, but not for me. I thought of penning down my emotion in my pocketbook. It was a warm feeling to know that your folks have finally arrived, with you and to your understanding. It's so relaxing to know that after a certain age, we accept each other, in a way that we could've never understood earlier.

'I've Arrived!

Away from the usual emotions
Foraying into the strangeness of ocean
Here I stand, far ahead & far beneath
Against those who knew not me, my frankness
My care and my love coated with nothing but sweetness

I am here again to reprise my song
I am here again to remind to that thought
I am here again to time travel while you're gone
I am here again to pinch and remind…

That I've arrived…in a land which not only stole my heart
But mirrored me back
That I've arrived, longing and surviving
Bidding goodbyes, and greeting new hi
That I've arrived like I'm reborn!'

The clock struck one in the afternoon, and it seemed I'd lost track of time while penning this down. This verse reminded me of my good times spent in London so much that I wished to meet a few unplanned people. However, the knock-on my door made me hurry as I knew it must be Bapa calling for an afternoon meal.

'Ma'am your parents have headed for a walk towards the central part, however, they said they'll not go too far, and have been provided with a map and a lot of advice. They didn't want you to be disturbed,' said the hotel assistant.

'Well, Mister, what can I do other than smiling at this!' I said and thanked him for passing on the information.

It was odd but also overwhelming to discover this side of my parents, this curious and explorative. I'd never found them as interesting as this, as adventurous as they are today. Maybe I misperceived them or was ignorant as I thought I knew more than them, or probably I avoided them as they were pushy about my marriage. Whatever be it, I felt great at their attempt to explore newness.

'Ruby…how are you, my mate?'

'Nayan, OMG…can't trust my senses, after ages, I thought you died!'

'Haahaaa, yeah ma'am, it's my ghost from the sub-continent! Great to know that you are still alive, and with London Theatre, ahem!'

'London Theatre would've been in ruins if I were not here. Needless to say, I am a supernova! Do I sound of having a superiority complex?'

I laughed out loud when I read her message. She didn't change, even for the goodness of God!

'Meet up? I am in Croydon!'

'Oh, damn! Damsel in distress is back! Of course, when and where, I'll text you back. After a while, it was decided that we would be catching up at 'Life in Secondhand', yeah, the same bookstore where we had first stumbled onto each other. She just opened a few loose knots, which I'd kept carefully when I'd decided to leave London for good!

The bookstore definitely stood away from the ones in that street, as renovation and modernization were at their peak. However, as per my old and stale beliefs, some things don't require modern intervention or renewals as they stand classy across all leaps of time. Such was the warm and tingling magic of 'Life in Secondhand'. I'd received the news of Mr Gabbai passing away, a year after I'd left London, to Birmingham, and then finally to the quaint little town of Rickmansworth. How time flies!

Rubail had cried cosily over the phone which had made me

quite uncomfortable and I'd taken the next train to London to bid a melancholic and musical farewell to her grandfather.

Mr Gabbai was inspiring in his sense of humour, the crude jokes on himself and people around, not even sparing me was remarkable. He was an actor in most senses possible, as he would enact his favourite novel's character by just setting up a mini-stage in the bookstore. He enjoyed the attention of others' when he showed his craft; he was a good critic, a great reader and a human being who had seen life and death from the closest inches possible. Their bookstore was so famous for its old collections and performing arts that it was even recognized by the city tourism guide book as a must-visit!

'He died in his sleep, smiling and happily,' sobbed a Rubail back then.

I remember this gentleman from nowhere, who, to a great extent had influenced my life, my writing. It was at his last ceremony that I'd met Ronnie for the final time if I can put it like that.

While thinking all of this wasn't easy, the city brought back a lot of memories old out of which I'd learnt a lot. Rubail texted again excusing herself for being a little late than usual. I had to wait. Shuffling books from one corner to another, I kept revisiting London several years back.

'I hear you've again fallen in love, poetess?' asked Mr Gabbai, smirking and winking his eyes at me.

'I don't know whether I can confirm that but…I was in love with someone back in India, when I was much younger and effervescent and that had great teachings, few heart-breaking events and I'm not sure Mr Gabbai, on whether or not I am in love. It's so complicated, love and its associated mirages.'

'Nayantara, my poetess, love is never complicated! Our thoughts towards it are, indeed, full of mazes. Love is in fact, very easy, very peaceful, extremely joyful, if you may kindly start observing, huh? Your needs are demanding and hence the emotional journey gets turmoiled. The associated relationship is complicated because humans are full of desire, demands, and self-obsessions! Love is selfless. With love comes greater spiritualism and responsibility, you become closer to nature, to the living, and also to the dead!'

'You are too kind and great to speak of it in such depth. How many may have retained that kind? Not sure, Mr Gabbai. The sustainability challenge always disturbs the energy of love. In the end, the energy fades, love fades. Hence, I am not sure about the remnants of feelings.' I looked away from him and he probably understood that I am hurt, emotional being.

'I have found my answers! We are fear-mongering people, Nayantara. We want Love to be mirrored as the exact version of our reflective thoughts, assumptions, accumulations over watching, and hearing. But that's being foolish, an idiot's trailer, to digress love.'

I was caught in his deep conversations. He had that charm and enigma to allure anybody into his conversation. May I say that he was a tiny version of Tagore! I drew an unbeatable portion of inspiration from him to write, to tell-tale my heart, which very few like him and Rubail had a heart for. And for the first time, I tried to explore the romantic emotion of Love- if I have exposed myself to love, so will I be exposed to pain! One doesn't come without another. And that exploration was calming to my rusty heart and unyielding mind.

Mr Gabbai could surely sense the turmoil of to-be or not-to-be that I was undergoing. Ronnie was but a man with desire. He had very honestly placed his choice with me. And ever since that meeting, my relationship with him had begun, on a very strange note, even without accepting his selfish needs. I constantly thought about him, his paranoia about physical importance, his concept of divinity, and his no strings attached fundamental; it was everything that I was not about. I realized that we were so different, such conflicting personalities, our wants, our concepts about love, about emotions, about each other were all running parallel and not congruent. However, there was the slightest 'we' about each other, a connection which we both couldn't avoid. Hence, even without being completely in agreement with it, I was giving it a thought, I was involved in it irrespective of it being a terrible misfit.

Did this mean I was a love-prone woman? Looking for somebody as indifferent and difficult as Ronnie? Culturally, emotionally & mentally, we didn't coincide! What would this futile relationship bring me, except failure! Hence, many thoughts were ballooning up in my mind. I was going berserk for sure, still considering his proposition of an intimate relationship. Knowing that we both would be miserable at it!

'Lost in Space, Madam Nayantara?'

The voice was one of the sexiest and happening that I'd missed for these many years! Yeah, the actress had arrived, my long-lost best friend had arrived.

29

RONNIE & RUBAIL

Where Ronnie was a hardcore self-loved man, Rubail was a carefree friend. You would call her a 3 am friend, a friend in need, a friend you can count on, a friend who'll share her opinion but will be around for sure. Ronnie was less brave, more conscious, worried about 'who might watch him' in public places, hence preferred his home and at lesser times mine. Rubail kept me in check that a man must like your bare soul before he just likes your bare body!

'A man isn't a man of love if he just falls in for your body and that's the man you've to be careful about!' is what she had exclaimed when she heard me seeing Ronnie.

'I don't expect love from him, Rubail.'

'Ultimately, you will. That's how women are created, their structuring and engineering is as such. It's difficult for this tribe to differentiate between physiological and psychological aspects. You mustn't deny that sex with love is the most vibrant than just sex with no love!'

I kept quiet and exactly knew what she was hinting at. I was in a non-acceptance mode. However, I hoped that Ronnie, if given some time, might believe in the emotional aspect of love and not just the physiological.

'Sometimes eyes don't reflect the mind, Nayantara. You know he just wants to fuck. And still, you are involved and I see that greatly. You are a believer in romance, love is your quality, you mustn't just sleep with a man for physicality as I foresee at the end, you'll be the affected one. Withdraw yourself before it's too late. Men like Ronnie, will only use convenience as their emotion! My dear, get out of that maze! You'll be hurt. Listen to the signs. And I am not sorry to confirm what you cannot accept.'

Rubail spoke and left that afternoon. It was real, her concern and care about me. But I didn't know if love was the thing I was expecting from Ronnie or anybody, neither sex. I had turned my back to it until his proposition included just the physical aspect. Ronnie had more drive than me. His midnight conversations were about getting in between my legs, and how much more he wanted to experiment with positions, and that I was too busy being shy and not letting him experiment. The first time we had it, it was awkward as in he was too nervous, so much that he could hardly turn hard. But indecisively, we did it. Not to deny that being a woman, kissing incessantly bought in some relief, some drive to take part in his insanely sexual saga. Once during the comforting foreplay, he uttered, 'My feelings wouldn't just stop for you…with time it wouldn't go!' Back at that delicate time, I wanted to confront him with, 'If you just want fuck, why the hell are you talking about feelings!' I couldn't ask. I couldn't be curt to him. Probably, my emotions were brewing, and I mistook his awkwardness in bed for care! Care for me and my comfort. However, post giving in to the physiological Gods of sex, I'd only heard him talk about us in bed, not romantically of course, but in very blunt and straight ways of just making that experience a lot more enjoyable, pleasurable. Not to forget that he kept my sexual hormones soaring with these talks and I'd quietly satisfied myself through it. Not being hypocritical here!

However, these temporary adjustments of sex didn't bring in a rain of relief in my life. As if my expectations from life were certainly not a man like Ronnie, who wouldn't succumb to anything but his joys and comforts, his moods and instances! Gradually, his prying talks about it most of the time made me rethink my approval of his stance in my life. A fewer times it was bothersome since while at work, he would hardly come forward and talk, and at other times, he would just cross the bridge of gap (self-created) and demand subtly to pay him attention, look in his eyes as if demanding for my care and attention. Earlier, in this disconnected relationship, I used to feel confused and dazed but after a while; I got this sorted! I realized that it was Ronnie, who was confused, his actions and words were seldom a match. He deterred his own words, escaped his own stand, always prioritized ego over humanity! I also in my mind had qualified him as a 'sadist' but didn't call out loud as I'd also discovered that I've begun liking a man who's not only insensitive but difficult and unpredictable in his stance with me. Sometimes, he would just delve into thinking about me, as he would put it across, and at other times, he would vehemently take me for granted; sometimes I would be his muse and likeness, and at others he would just wrap it up by saying, 'It's short-term!' He was in a particular pattern that I'd identified and was glad but I couldn't withdraw myself from him! I got connected with a man who I couldn't love or stay with! Irony!

As time passed by, we had had too many differences, cold wars, and non-syrupy sagas. It was already a year and a half, but yet the fragmented relationship that he called 'friendship' didn't bring in any peace within. I couldn't vouch for him on this, and neither could I discover a sweet friend in him. He was never there for me if I could sum it up! But I was so accommodated to this broken affair that I wanted to be there for him, around, as a friend, caring and listening to his state of heart. He shared nothing discreet or valuable to me. I just knew that flowers put him off, and also that he didn't prefer calling me by names, no dears or darlings! I was chained by his thoughts, and I didn't want to address a flimsy affair as love. Love is what we never shared!

Rubail was right when she said that only sex means no good! And that I would get hurt. I was scared in confirming to her I had been hurt by this man on several occasions, purposely or not, I was! And each time, he would write something emotional, I would forget about his cold heart and ignore his callous behaviour and give him another chance. Hence, even I had developed a pattern, unable to walk away from this bitter/unstill attraction, no matter how distanced I was, how ignorant I became. Its tentacles wouldn't leave me, is when I had discovered by chance that I was in a karmic soup-a karmic relationship.

I think it was the month of June 2009, when Ronnie tried reaching out to me and Rubail had asked me to try as much as possible to avoid his request. 'Try harder to not meet him. Let your heart be as stubborn as it wants to be, train your mind to not give in.' This time I thought of listening to my friend rather than my wandering heart. I didn't answer many of his calls, which was very unlikely of my pattern. He had texted me to meet at the same place where we had first met. Yes! London's 44, I was so tempted at his request because it wasn't often, he had wanted to meet in a public place. Probably, he changed his course of thinking about us! I was a little optimistic in allowing him the benefit of the doubt and not jumping to conclusions. My impulsive-self wanted to nod to his request immediately. He said that he wanted to share something important, something that might elate me. I was excited and couldn't contain it. And I immediately texted him back saying yes. He added to the conversation by asking me to meet him at his apartment on the same evening. I accepted that too. Without confirming the same to Rubail, I tried taking conflictive decisions that I knew would certainly affect me soon. I was being nothing but a fool!

On being carried away, I reserved a table at the pub since it was a Saturday evening and people drool over places like these. I wanted to surprise him by also asking for a champagne but reserved it for the moment. Counting days, it was Friday evening, and I texted him by asking him if six in the evening would suit him on a Saturday. He didn't respond. My calls went unanswered too! Not knowing what was to be done, I kept waiting with patience.

It was an afternoon of the decided to date and I, with all my anger made it to London's 44 pub. The table was by the open space, where one could view the street, and also see people departing, embracing each other, kissing passionately, some to return and some to go forever, for good. My loneliness that evening didn't make me weep but made me angry, to a level of being foolish in this entire season of a void relationship. It pissed me off. I was more to be blamed as I repetitively made room for him, which he didn't deserve!

With agitation lingering around me and karma biting me at its highest shriek, I chucked him out of my life with all my attitude. I knew he was an egocentric devil, hence I wanted to text him my final message, 'Good riddance! I am done with this nonsense.' After texting him, I was still mad at myself for having relied on a man who was not humane at all, who always placed his needs over mine; who didn't leave a chance to hurt me! His intentions were clear and so were mine. After a zapped year and a half, I had realized and I wanted my free thoughts to celebrate.

I'd shared with Rubail about my lackadaisical approach to life. She'd said nothing but a warm welcome. I asked her for some advice because back then; I was nothing but vulnerable, agitated over my poor decision making. She called me that evening irrespective of being in-between her stage show and said, 'Quit London. Explore Britain. Breathe out. Stay Still.'

Alas! I'd followed her words of wisdom and no matter how dear London was to me in these many years, I'd kissed it a goodbye!

'Quitting your beauty
Will surely make my heart fidgety
Will surely create ripples of uncertainty

But O my mistress
My love will be for eternity
Till I return, I'll hold you tight in my thoughts
And never leave a sigh without thinking about our intensity!'

So, my journey has been forever in the British Islands, I have been roaming from Glasgow in the north to Wales in the west but nowhere it has been as memorable as London, even the close proximity of

Birmingham couldn't instill any warmth until I finally settled down in the quaint little town of Rickmansworth, which by far has been settling to me, not to forget the wonderful company of Mrs Patrick and then her lovely daughter, Nicole.

186

Birmingham couldn't instill any warmth until I finally settled down in the quaint little town of Rickmansworth, which by far has been settling to me, not to forget the wonderful company of Mrs Patrick and then her lovely daughter, Nicole.

30

WE MEET AGAIN AT CROYDON'S

'Yes Ma'am, the first screening of the manuscript will take 3 weeks to 8 weeks and if you don't hear from us, which means better luck next time!'

'Hold on! What percent of chance does an Asian writer hold in your agency? She's new but very skilful. Huh?' inquired Nicola hurriedly.

'Can't really comment on that but if she's really good, place of origin doesn't come under consideration at all! And Writer's & Poet Ltd. is all about allowing new poets and writers to find their literary place.'

'Thank you, Ma'am! Helps me a lot!'

Nicola after a long pause clapped both her hands together and giggled out of excitement. She was quite nervous about calling up the agency. She has a lot to thank to Mr Cunningham and Bella! However, Mister Cunningham hasn't stopped calling her since that bashful event of Veronica. Although the calls were more regular than extraordinarily imposing, it was demanding for her to answer, and she avoided any confusion when it came to men. She's had a lot of flurries in her life, self-created, all of it and now she was tired of it herself. Wanted to control her heart and mind out of it, which she was succeeding at! But undeniably, she was strikingly beautiful, which often led men to fall for her beauty, and she was quite aware of the fact that she was; however, today it seemed a hindrance to the pursuit of her life's goal. Sometimes, she missed the passionate turmoil of emotions, when the blood refuses to relax, and the body temperature was too high and ready to give in to the hormones, to the insanity of pleasure, but she has come a long way to calm it down by just sitting by herself and looking at the galaxy of stars outside her window. She speaks to them often. They know her- the blend of her needs and wishes.

But it relaxes her, breathes her fine, and that's how she's been treating such upheaval. And has no complaints about it.

She'd met Bella the next weekend and shared the news of her dream come true publication success. Bella wanted to take her to Starbucks and treat her to an espresso and a bagel which was quite famous for a humble celebration. 'May I ask Eddie to join us? He stays two blocks away!' 'Your client or friend, Bella?' 'Huh! Really, you that blonde, eh?' Nicola wasn't surprised at Bella's sudden attempt to include her friend, as she was always fond of company. Focusing on the bagel, she wasn't quivered at Bella's work talk and customer experiences.

There I saw Mr Cunningham strolling casually to the coffee joint! And my espresso just turned cold! Looking at Bella, I gave her a sharp little scorn but she in return smiled sheepishly as if it's her duty to hook me up! 'Hey, Rose! You look so good today!' Bella got up from her seat and offered it to Mr Cunningham and excused herself to get another one. In the meantime, I was dazed and utterly confused and greeted him very softly. He looked at me and passed an extremely sweet smile. I couldn't return the same passion and continued having the cold espresso. The weather was just so fine and he was humming a song by Lobo. It was so awkward as I couldn't reciprocate with any of his sweetness. He asked suddenly, 'Who's your favourite musician or band?' I said, 'George Michael,' in a hurry and waited for Bella to join us fast as I didn't want both of us to be left by ourselves. Thankfully, Bella returned with an Iced Tea for Eddie! Duh me! He was called Eddie, Eddie Cunningham! And some more convolutions, eh!

'Eddie Burlington Cunningham was a smart-looking gentleman, sporting a salt and pepper look with dark-rimmed-thick glasses to shape his long face quite fine. He was a brunette, thankfully, and in no meaning literal! A relaxing, settled mind, observant and friendly, sweet temperament with a heart-melting smile. His overlapping left-side tooth, though a result of dental negligence but it seemed so right sitting on his face. Just about 175 cm in height, he was nothing but an unconventional wonder not only to the eyes but one's company!' Nicola's thoughts preceded her surroundings and she found meeting with Eddie full of profundity! But she didn't bring it up on her expressions as Bella was watching over her like an eagle. Any of it and she would be caught up in her match-fixing net! Hence, Nicola went plain with her expressions this time.

No sooner it was past six in the evening and the weather turned a little breezy, slightly giving out the chills and a need for a shawl or a jacket! Nicola had none and Eddie offered his! Bella sighed, 'Oh Lordy Lord!' and giggled. Certainly, Bella out of all the friends that Nicola has had was the best. Matured, playful, delightful, joyful, and encouraging. She must be around 20 years older than her, but Bella's life seemed far more exciting, fun-filled, and responsible than Nicola's. Hence, she couldn't deny her proposal to go to Eddie's small gathering the next weekend. And Bella was a true friend, she had something on her mind! She was friends to Eddie, long before she knew Nicola or her plight.

Eddie belonged to the great business family of the Burlington Looms Ltd. The Burlington's were the official fabric provider to Her Highness since the time of Elizabeth I, nearly for five hundred-odd years! The family's legacy spreads across the west of England to the scenic island of Scotland. The family, although of Scottish origin, was one of the first businesses to decide to go merge when Burlington gave away part of its shares to Reddit linens post World War I, when the entire English land was devastated and running their mills into a drastic closure. The times were toughest for the family to survive and continue their legacy for their future generations. Then Eddie's grandfather, who was quite an outspoken non-orthodox Englishman, generated an idea to keep maximum share to Burlington, and partial to Reddit Linens in 1935. Reddit Linens was an American establishment, headquartered in New York city.

The merger saved them! However, the legendary loom was sharing its prestigious name with an American mill. Many of the conservatives in England protested, including a few in the family. Thirty years of an exhaustive internal battle, finally, Eddie's elder uncle could bring back the family's cultural & financial heritage to the Burlington's yet again, but with much trials and tribulations. There was merry making and the entire family was in a celebratory mood when Eddie's parents had proudly announced their first parenthood. Hence, Eddie, peculiarly, is considered as an extremely good omen for the Burlington family. Eddie takes care of the Eastern & East midland of the business. Not denying that London is a huge market which is still taken care of by his father and Uncles.

'It's an inspiring story! He must be a nice man. But I don't understand why I'd to be walked down through this story?' asked a confused Nicola.

Bella sighed and bowed down. 'Maybe there's a bright tomorrow waiting for you with a great partner.'

Nicola couldn't stop looking at Bella's sincere efforts to hitch her up, thinking about her wellbeing that few of her mates had thought through. She was astounded by her sisterly instincts and care.

With silence and happiness of being cared for, she carried on to her tiny apartment. Bella had requested a Saturday outing at Eddie's place and she was still unsure about it. Scott was on her mind. His proposal, his craziness, his burden…and it seemed she was unsure about him too. Hence, she called the day off and went off to bed with Adrian's thoughts only.

'Like hell, what made you think about one of the busiest markets in London?' asked an exasperated Rubail with a black at the corner of her mouth.

'Since when are you this unsocial about busy sites, huh, actress?' I nudged her.

'Since you left London, grandpa left for his after-life and I left seeking love!'

I stopped as if my heart skipped a beat after the revelation. She evaded looking at me and kept smoking. The look on her face was not too grave, it was accustomed to the dreariness of being alone, of constantly reminding that one is contented; that it's life! But I have experienced that the only way of remaining truthful to oneself is to just keep going, of never evading the reality and that only a few will bring you a smile. You've to do it for yourself. Not many will feel your fingers, see you the way that you are. You've to see 'you' for yourself!

I patted at Rubail's shoulders which had become muscular and I complimented her, 'Toned, eh!' 'Yes, poetess!' We giggled and walked into the busy lane of Croydon.

Croydon was a place as crowded as it ever could be. But we had our space in that too. Quite often, in earlier days, much younger than what we are to this day when London showed me hope and horizons of possibility, the struggling artist, Rubail, and a regular banking employee evaded the world and found peace in this quaint little joint called Tea Stalkers. Few footfalls here as it was not that 'cool' a joint for youngsters. It was for regulars like us. As we stepped in, thoughts of Mr Gabbai crept in as he would usually consider this place as a struggling man's haven. He never considered himself old enough, mentally he wasn't yet. Mr Gabbai would refer to me as an aunt from the land of spiritualism. He had an eagerness to visit India like every other westerner but could never make it. Ironically, Rubail was never that fond of travelling to unknown lands. Like always, she preferred staying, growing, and dying here in London, until her theatrical acts made a tour of other geographies. She was '*sthai*' like the trees and I had titled her the *sthai mitzvah* of all commandments.

'You look great but you've put on some pounds. Must I compliment, my poetess,' giggled as she talked.

'Oh! that's great and also a warning to slim down, I assume.'

'You can take it in a way you like it. I ordered our old favourite Darjeeling tea!'

'You remember?'

'Most things!'

'I am planning to publish my poems and turn into a full-time writer.'

'Still planning that? I thought you must have been by now.'

'I wanted to earn first. Get financial securities. Now I have a house without any loan on it, a car, a great caretaker, hired an assistant for arranging my manuscript and organizing my calendar. I think I am ready now. Not to forget, I was successful in getting my folks along with me to London. I would pursue them to settle here, with me as they are turning older. I think now I am ready as I am settled.'

'I am so glad! Any boyfriend?' and she winked.

'After the debacle of Jojo in India and Ronnie in London, I am not ready for any steady relationship. It requires a lot of effort to deal with another ego. I am flustered by the thought of it even.'

'Seriously, no sex for that long! Don't ridicule me!'

'As my biological needs are different and sorted from the rest of mankind, you are right, I just can't have lame sex with anyone.'

'Good lecture, but no offense. I get you totally. Even I am out of those frivolous exchanges. And cheers to that!'

'I was seeing somebody, but I foresee even that'll not work out. Too many dissimilarities.'

'Hah! You bet as we grow up, we become so much aware of our needs and desires that it's okay not to chase after these meaningless fornications…fuck them all Nayan!'

We laughed, talking about Rubail's experiences in the theatres and her narrow sexual escapades and about her fandom in London theatres and how she has made a handful of great mates.

'Nayan, however, Ronnie is still in touch with me and fewer times has asked about your whereabouts. Sorry, if it's a spoiler!'

'What! Why?'

'Somehow, he had my number and one fine evening called me up, sounding flushed, and wanted to meet you in person. I avoided telling him about you. It's been almost five years to that when you were in Wales, I guess.'

'I am extremely grateful to you.'

'Also, that he took an off and headed to Prague and was working there for four years until he returned to London, then retreated to Rockwood, his family, and gave up his banking career. He's said to start a business that promotes veganism.'

'Wow, so much has happened! Good for him! And you were in touch? Applause for that!'

'You jealous huh, aren't you?'

I smiled, and she winked at me. 'Let's hit the bar tomorrow, what say?'

'Alright then…let's hit the bar tomorrow? Before that, join me for brunch tomorrow? With my family?'

'Whoa…okay…sure! Tell me what to wear?'

'Doesn't matter!'

'I've read that many Indian parents don't like either their offspring or it's friends with skin-revealing outfits.'

'Wear something nice and suitable please if you are aware.'

31

BACK AND FORTH

*'**B**ack in a month*
Where the sun was shining bright
And hues had mounted the skylight
And all I knew was waiting for you…

You'd turned your back
Giving me that sarcastic laugh
Escaping through the narrowest lanes
And pricking me till my coldest veins…

I was stranded
And you were too proud!'

'Nayan, open the door,' knocked my mother at the door.

I had to rush my brain from the dysfunctional stories of Ronnie to the reconciled bond between my parents. 'Yes, Maa!' and I rushed to the door.

We both rushed to her room as my folks had literally shopped the hell out of London. I couldn't find a spot empty in that motel room. 'Ah…what've you guys done? Shopping or looting?'

'I've shopped after ages! Let's agree your dad has not only been an orthodox Hindu but also a miserly person. But today, I retaliated and argued with him like never. Got all the necessary or unnecessary things ever.'

'She hardly understands that rupees and pounds have different values and pounds are certainly cutting my pocket. I don't work anymore. I have my pension funds. But wives, are they even bothered?'

'Oh! C'mon it's not like I'll come to London often and shop. So, stop whining and start enjoying this ride of foreign soil. I am on a roll, Buli! And I must thank you for fulfilling my life's dream. I feel so great here!'

'Ok, Bapa, I'll compensate for your losses. And Ma, there are chances that you can have this enjoyment forever! Next, when you both come down, it'll be a forever settlement. We'll talk about it elaborately once we reach Rickmansworth.'

My mum wasn't listening as she was lost in the deep sea of colours, designs and accessories. I, too, submerged myself in her shopping escapades. After an hour later, we both discovered that shopping is nothing but fun. And also, my parents had a ball out there. Observing their nags currently were funny as I didn't pay any heed or took any of it seriously. It's lifelong for them, and they were habituated to it. Hence, I didn't interfere either.

'Ma, tomorrow a very dear friend of mine will join us for brunch. So, you guys can take ample rest for the day. You must be jet-lagged.'

'Alright, what's his name? Is he a Hindu? Indian?'

'Calm down Ma. It's just a friend named Rubail. And not everybody is an Indian here,' I smiled and wished them both Goodnight, suggesting to opt for room service.'

My folks smiled out of a sense of relief as it wasn't a guy, ironically, they also seemed a little worried as it wasn't a guy!

Rubail's attire was more on the funnier side than chic! I must agree that the gesture was quite warm to opt for an Indian outfit, however, the choice of clothing was hideous. And I just nudged her over the dramatic lehenga choli look with all north Indian marriage accessories.

She and my mother had communication problems as Mom didn't know English properly and she didn't understand Odia. My dad struck a terrific chord with Rubail talking about Odia theatres and his fondness for it. How he used to lie at home and skip his lectures a couple of times a week to attend plays. Rubail was too enthralled by his stories. After all, he was a walking & talking story from India. My mother tried her best to involve herself but failed miserably. I was glad that they received Rubail this well.

Before she left, she bowed with a humble 'Namaste' and invited my parents for her weekend play.

My father nodded, as he was too excited to be a part of something new. On seeing my father's enthusiasm, my mother was spirited too! And I was very joyful as it was a great moment to be cherished. Hence, we took a lot of pictures that day.

Rubail requested me to stay back until the weekend so that my folks could witness her play. I instantly agreed because she will perform at the London theatre. My mother promised Rubail that she'll bring her a memorable present.

Nicola was on cloud nine. Nayantara's manuscript of poem collection was accepted. And the publication was interested to sign a contract with the new poet. She had represented herself as her assistant, which didn't make things easy at all. What made it easier for a non-Brit to publish her collection in such a short time was 9% luck and 91% Eddie Cunningham! Nicola couldn't thank him enough. 'He was kind', she thought. 'I must give him something nice this Saturday.'

It was Saturday and Bella like any other good friend reminded her of Eddie's small gathering to which Nicola confirmed her participation. She had bought a book of P.B Shelley that she thought might interest Eddie. Very caringly, she wrapped it in a reusable paper adding a note of appreciation. Nicola was a beautiful woman, but she wasn't too focused on accoutred ways, hence her appearances were always simpler than her looks. And post her debacle with Scott, she preferred to keep things as a plain jane would. Hence, clamouring herself in something glamourous would be nothing but conflictive.

'What took you so long?'

'Oh! I was thinking what to wear as it would be an elitist's gathering, hence was shuffling through my wardrobe.'

'And? You adorned this?' asked a baffled Bella.

'Something wrong with this dress? Mother gifted me this on my first anniversary!'

'Very emotional that is, but sorry to say that this is too outdated and simple for his party,' cried Bella.

'Party? I thought it's a small gathering? You are making me nervous. You never opposed my dressing style at Veronica's huge party, huh?'

'Oh! Good Lord! I can't explain the difference!'

'Now who's delaying?'

'Fine! Let's trot away with this topic!'

'Let go of my fashion sense. I know it's ghastly. Please, Bella.'

'Never mind. But your next shopping trip is with me.'

Okay as she assured, they took a cab to Eddie's small haven, as he had described last time. Certainly, it was not small! Nicola was taken by a storm at his palatial condo and felt very uncomfortable to take her steps further. All her life, no friend of hers had a place like that. Everybody was brought up modestly, in moderation, like her. So, this drastic affluence and its association seemed unnecessary, out of purview, and she suddenly stopped at the main door. It was five in the evening, the surrounding nature had retired, the only people living their lives were us, humans and strangely, Nicola anticipated the entire evening to be a set-up, and wanted to vanish with the click of fingers. 'I want to leave! Now!' 'Are you alright? What happened to you suddenly?' 'Not feeling right about anything that's happening?' Nicola stopped a cab nearby and without explaining herself further left the venue.

On reaching her tiny apartment, she noticed that it brought nothing but comfort to her again. It wasn't on Nicola's cards to just blend into any kind. The sudden disappearance from Eddie's party was insanely discourteous, but she contemplated that maybe that was the best she could do. With Scott's proposal already dwindling her into tiny fragments of guilt, she didn't want yet another band of romantic diaspora. Hence, she thought ignorance and clinging onto herself was a better remedy than being responsive to these changes and demands.

With these thoughts, she stewed a cup of vegetable soup to relax her nerves. Bread was already baked in the morning, hence, after having her supper, she waited for the clock to strike 7 pm so that she could call Adrian and her mother.

Mrs Patrick hung up the phone and cuddled Adrian, who was kept away from her natural mother for almost four months now. She was getting older. Managing two pet dogs and Adrian was a challenge, but she never succumbed to it as she was the mountaineer lady, Gustavia. Few thoughts scattered brought her back to thinking she might have been too strict with Nicola., she was an adult and had the right to choose her life but sincerity is what she had expected from her as that was the most effective trait of her father. He was a sincere and dedicated man, hence was loved across the ranges. Amidst the thoughts, she received a call from Nayantara stating that her plans for Rickmansworth were delayed as they were staying back for Rubail's play.

'Sure, Nayan! It's been long, and I have missed you.'

'I miss you too, my caring lady! Do you want anything from London?'

'Ah…I'll text you once I've decided. Thanks for asking.'

'Wait, don't hang up. Convey Nicola that I've got something exciting for her!'

'Sure!' as she hesitantly said, she had a drop of a tear rolling down in the abyss. Flashback of her daughter's unforgiven act of intolerant nature got her. What would she explain to Nayantara! Trust was compromised and so was the promise devalued. Nayantara would eventually find out about the dastardly act...but even Scott, he's not a gentleman for her. He cheated on her. These unscrupulous facts of the past worried her, and she didn't know whether to confess or keep quiet. Both would be eruptions-one within and another outside! On remembering Gustav and holding on to her current strength, she stayed silent as that was the most honest thing that she could think of; do rather! Taking the armchair at the study, she rested with Adrian on her lap and Elsa and Nelsa by her side.

32

THE SOLITARY REAPER

Although my mother couldn't map the philosophy behind Rubail's play, which was about climate change and its repercussions on animals of all kinds-even humans, she didn't evade away from congratulating her. It was for the very first time that we could explore the greatness of the London Theatre. The auditorium was a piece of art fulfilling a capacity of 250 seated enthusiastic audience. The monument was very highly regarded amongst artists of all genres, and it was Mr Gabbai's dream stage. He'd always encouraged anybody pursuing fine arts to have laborious struggles of making it to the London Theatre. It was an extremely prestigious moment for his granddaughter to have made it through her arduous dreams. As a friend, I couldn't be happier, as I saw the audience cheering and applauding their way throughout. My father was quite excited to be there to witness something so different than the plays of his time.

'Thank you so much for appreciating this. It was a play written with a lot of dreams involved and finally, we could present it!'

'A passionate heart's tale never misses striking a chord,' said my father.

'Here, this is for you! From my Indian fashion wardrobe,' said Mom in her unprecedented English.

Rubail's heart was filled with joy as she accepted it and embraced my mother in a jest thanking her for a zillion times.

'It's time for you both to also acknowledge that your daughter, Nayantara has been writing poems ever since she was studying in Goa! You didn't know about that? Did you?'

I looked at Rubail. My parents looked at me stunned, literally taken aback! Hence, we all ended up looking at each other with awkwardness. There was a long pause and just the silence and the walk towards a nearby Lebanese restaurant called, Hunger Karam! Rubail's one of the most favourite dining spots.

The situation of awkwardness was eluded when there were few folk singers in the restaurant. My father strictly stuck to vegetarian food as he didn't want to try meat of any sort. Rubail stuck to her regular item kibbeh, and I was just having some pita bread with tabbouleh wherein my parents dug into it from time to time.

'Let me unwrap the gift, Mrs Pani.'

'Sure, Rubail!'

'Oh my…it's a sari!' she blushed out of happiness and holding my mothers' hands, she said, 'thank you!'

My mom was too joyous to unveil her happiness and asked me to explain to her the handlooms of Odisha silk.

'I'll teach you how to drape a sari,' I said.

'Sure!'

My parents invited Rubail to Puri and then Rickmansworth! Both two scattered pieces of land in the history of civilization. I grinned, and she embraced my parents. My father was a little awkward since we rarely embrace each other in my family. Historically, I have never encountered my parents cuddling each other or even holding hands, hence embracing, kissing each other was not at all a family culture. However, I saw my dad cope up in this extreme exchange of cultures, and was kind of glad he didn't tail a hypocritical Indianism with him to this foreign soil.

The next morning, we boarded a train to Rickmansworth and Rubail promised to come over. In these many years, she'd never dropped by my place, which may sound stranger than it appears to be! However, that didn't affect our friendship. Apparently, distance, work, or even a state business never dissuades you to like a person as reality never tricks, it presents exactly how things are! Rubail was a dear friend and no matter which part of earth she would've been, nothing could've failed our reality. This was the only reality that didn't bewitch me over these years. Or else I truly sucked in relationships.

'He knows you stopped by!'

'C'mon, why did you tell him? And what does he want after so many years! Huh?'

'He wants to meet you! Not aware why, actually, after a decade literally and it seems he still likes you!'

'Crap! You take care!'

'I never liked him as he was a cold piece of shit and you a jewel of emotions. I still don't like him, but the way he insisted made me think twice about it. One meeting and then you can sing your sonnet of goodbye, huh?'

'I don't know. I'll think about it. I need to board now.'

Rubail messaged me his contact number, which I ignored royally. Post breaking up with him, his strangeness and callousness got onto me in a way greater than my happiness. His unfair bond with me made me too sceptical to get into a real relationship. It was as if he had snatched away all my happy state of being, and very foolishly I had allowed it. Allowed him to be unfair, treat me like a thing of pleasure. And no feelings got into his thick skin! I put on my earplugs for some music but his mention brought unpleasant memories. The only recreational reinforcement was me getting into poetry again.

'You brought a place in the apartment, right?'

'No Bapa, it's an individual residence. I'd told you and Ma before the purchase, right? I got it at a fair deal when a Norwegian family moved to their homeland, and were looking for suitors in a scurry and I had turned into a spendthrift in that small town of Rickmansworth; one of my mates in real estate business had imposed me to buy this! And there I had invested around 25k pounds to purchase this. Working in a bank helped!'

'Great move…one must invest in real estate, whichever location!'

'We are so proud of you, Buli,' said my mother looking completely different in her changed avatar!

'Thank you!'

'Four months and it feels like a year! It's so good to see you!' Mrs Patrick embraced me so dearly that I could feel my parents puzzling reactions to it. 'Mr and Mrs Pani, welcome to your daughters' home. It's so good to finally meet you both.' My mother shook hands since she could only utter a thank you. My father with his best accent greeted Mrs Patrick.

'I have made Indian bread and paneer makhani,' said an excited Mrs Patrick.

'You didn't have to do that,' I said with a smile on my face.

Meanwhile, my folks were busy checking the house which they considered smaller but beautifully placed. They loved the neighbourhood, the yard, the small garden, the walkway outside, the adjacent park, and the weather. 'Hold on, till it fluctuates!' 'Does it happen often?' asked my father to which I nodded big time.

'You folks seem to be quite inquisitive, isn't it?'

'Yes, I know why. They are in a comparative mode. Comparing it to my house in India!'

'Parents after all!'

'Huh ah…Indian parents!' as I said I nudged Mrs Patrick.

The dinner was sumptuous, although not that spicy like the

actual curry but very well-tried. I had insisted Mrs Patricks complete dining with us but she was in a hurry as her hounds must wait for her. My father seemed to be a little dazed by seeing her protective side towards her pets. 'Mr Pani, a mother of one can be a mother for all!' said Mrs Patrick and smiled. My father laughed heartily and requested her to tag her pets along for tomorrow's morning stroll. It felt great to be able to finally have a surrounding that brought peace. Wishing Mrs Patrick goodnight, my parents wanted to rest as they were too exhausted from the journey, not denying their old age too.

Very strangely, I didn't find Nicola around and hence texted her. Post that I retired to my study and picked up a book that least interested me as my mind kept wandering about various events of the past. 'Rubail shouldn't have given me Ronnie's number.'

The morning was filled with great sunlight, a little warmer than usual and while watering the plants, she didn't want to get late for work. The mobile seemed to drain out the battery. Putting it on charge, she got busy getting ready.

The library started exactly at 7:30 am and there she was still at home, struggling to get her things arranged, and she hardly understood the reason for her being late. 'What's up with me!' outraged Nicola and left in a jiffy. 'Finally!' she cried to herself and was irritated for getting late for no reason. The head librarian interrogates people who are late, and she didn't want to face him at the start of her day. She kept whispering as much as nagging to herself. Thankfully, she was saved as the head librarian was on a leave himself. Thanking her stars, she continued filling the new books that had been piling for a long time. Her state of work took over and no sooner she forgot to check her messages.

Around fifteen minutes past ten, she realized that she wanted to drink a beverage and her phone rang.

'Hey, you! Good morning!'

'Ah...hello Mister Cunningham, what a surprise!' she said being unsure.

'Yeah! The last meeting was rather awkward anyways, I had work with O&M Mills, it's around the corner and the person in charge might take a little more time to meet. Would you mind a cup of tea, provided the weather is cloudy and warm at the same time?'

'I?' she iterated with uncertainty.

'Do you mind if we walk down? There's a sweet little Asian tea-stall around the corner.'

'Sure, let me bring my umbrella.'

They both strolled, maintaining their distance. There was an awkward silence as Nicola felt guilty for not showing up at his place, and also because the meeting was happening without Bella. 'Call me Eddie. It's sweet and short!'

Nicola giggled, 'Sure, Eddie! How about that?'

'Perfect Madam!'

'How's your friends' book coming along?'

'Actually, she's my mom's employer but is a very sweet and inspiring lady. She's working on it.'

'Amazed that you are helping her out!'

'I am her personal assistant!'

'Great!' He stopped right at the corner of the lane where there was a diversion and with very few onlookers. I don't want to sound desperate but how about us? Let me be absolutely honest with you. I'd like you since that party. Hence, I was looking for a chance to speak to you. Try me! I'll not disappoint you. I believe in monogamy and I am looking for a partner. I've found that balance in you. You are the one for me!'

Nicola was quiet as she could expect it coming someday, but Bella not being by her side was odd. Let's just say she got goose bumps.

'Let me allow you some days to think over it. This weekend, I'll wait for your reply. And yes, it's a proposal, quite unromantic but from my heart.'

Nicola's discomfort surmounted, but yet she lived up to be a polite girl. She decided to visit her mother for a few days and narrate the entire episode, as much like mend her relationship with her mother. Scott and now Eddie! Must be her karma for sure.

'I'll share a great news, Mother! And please convey my regards to Nayantara. Let her know that the manuscript is with me.' She hung up the phone. She was glad that finally, her gift to Nayantara is nothing but turning into a robust plan. Dazed with proposals of getting married, she headed to Rickmansworth for some divine silence and space.

33

SONNETS TO PARADISE

Nayantara's version of Nicola's sudden decision to return to Leicester was like a flash in the pan, as she had expected her to submerge in the work of her manuscript. Everything was haphazard from that front, as out of nowhere, she had vanished into herself, and on top of it without Adrian. The situation seemed way too absurd for Nayantara to believe that Nicola had left just like that.

'Who is Nicola, Buli?' asked my dad.

'She's Mrs Patrick's daughter, an intelligent yet unstill person. Beautiful yet non-prudent. Ambitious yet clueless!'

'That's a world apart. Can one person be all of that? Wonderful aspects of humans, huh?' he smirked.

'Yes, Bapa, nothing but wonderful.'

'By the way, I've taken the day off so we all go sightseeing.'

'I like it at home. Take your mother. She'll be thrilled but no more shopping, please.'

I wanted all of us to hang out together, but it seemed as if my father was enjoying the window view, Mrs Patrick's English teas, and

Elsa & Nelsa's company better than sightseeing. He was reluctant and hence stayed back.

Post checking the pastry shop, we headed out to the summer farmer market at Bee's Produce. My mother was keen on checking English vegetables out of the blue! The market was a veggie's delight if I must agree, and my mother being a vegetarian found it amusing. She shuffled, squatted, leaned, bent on her knees, checked the carrots meticulously, the turnips fussily, the shallots surprisingly and the actions of her peculiarity continued. I headed to a make-shift noodle soup stall and ordered two bowlfuls of delight. Looking around, I found the weather to be pleasant enough to just calm and stretch to happiness.

'Hi Naads,' a heavy voice interrupted.

And it was odd, bad, and I was awestruck to find none other than him by my side, smiling as if we were long-lost friends!

'Hello,' my voice lost all its charm.

Scott sprung up in my life when I had least wanted or expected him. His sudden and cold treatment in my haven in the winters was unforgiven. Yet he showed up like some unnecessary piece of news. And at this juncture, I was not ready for his apologies or friendship.

'Distance doesn't mean I've forgotten us.'

'Doesn't matter what it means!'

'I clearly get that. But we can call it a truce. Forget our mishappening and continue as people who just know each other.'

'I am not in a frame of mind to process all that information. If you could excuse me.'

'I don't understand the reason for us being in this situation. Did Nicola tell you something?'

'Nicola? Why involve her? What role she has to play in your misgivings?'

Scott realized and thanked his star for Nicola not disclosing their alleged affair. Also, he was looking for an opportunity to bring it up. When and how he seemed unsure.

'Your folks are here!'

'And you are spying on me? Are you a spy?'

'Yes, I am.'

He sighed and left the conversation at that, but I had a feeling that he met me for some purpose. Only he could know the reason. He left the market immediately.

She was fidgety as she kept fiddling with her carry-bag multiple times. 'Yes, it's there. So, is the book's contract letter. Nothing else. I forgot nothing else.' Before leaving for Rickmansworth, she had texted Bella stating that she'll be out for a week, and also for some reason she did text Eddie too. 'I'll be back with an answer. Going to meet my mother and Nayantara.'

Puffing and swindling, the exhalation wouldn't stop as a fewer time the guilt of having got involved with Scott would keep her perched awkwardly. She would immediately wipe her face, but not even a drop of perspiration. She exhaled a lot many times as she had finally decided not to marry Scott and bring more shame to her employer and mostly her mother. 'My mistake. My actions and my fate are all aligned now.' Uttering those, she got down from the train and very nervously picked up her suitcase till she had reached the bus stop. The weather very swiftly turned from sunny to cloudy, as if she brought the withering clouds with her. She got onto a bus and yet again checked her bag, just to be sure whether her most astounding gift to Nayantara was safe or not!

'Nayan, I've arrived! And there awaits a surprise for you.' She texted in a haste.

At home, it was a perfect scene of a vegetarian feast, as Ma was too occupied in arranging and rearranging the vegetables. She wanted to invite my friends over, but it was too difficult to explain to her that my colleagues stayed in another place. I assured her of Nicola's arrival but she was cooking for 10 people and wanted everyone to taste a delightful Odia meal. My father was zoned out in this meddlesome afternoon where my mother kept asking me for her help. I was so flustered at the end of it I wanted to take a nap in the study. I shut the door and requested nobody to disturb me.

I sat in peace and no sooner checked the number forwarded to me by Rubail. Ronnie's number. Looking at it didn't change the order and neither the name attested to it. It was his contact number and he wanted me to have it. Why! I still kept pondering. Several years passed by, and he couldn't drop in a line of concern and now all he had to do was advocate his dilemma through my friend. It certainly was annoying. I sighed and while toggling the screen got notified by Nicola's arrival and no sooner fell asleep.

'What are you doing here? Like always…you are so sudden and abruptly appear and re-appear…and mom can be here any minute! Just go away!'

'Is this a kind of treatment you give to people who love you? Huh?'

'I am sorry but we decided not to meet again! And you suddenly turn up…even Nayantara is around!'

'I know. I met her today.'

'Then what do you want from me?'

'Let's tell Naads the truth about us and be free of any guilt.'

'Never. I've hurt my mother enough in this life and I am not going to iterate the shameful act to Nayantara…of all people! Are you out of your mind?'

'No, it's important for us to be honest. Whether or not we get married, we must disclose what's there between us to her. And of all people, she's the one who must know.'

'Her folks have come down from India, and all you think is about yourself! How unkind of a heart is that, Scott?'

'You can judge me, but let's tell her.'

'You must go from here, right now!'

'Eventually, I will my dear, as the Interpol has plans to shift me to Spain for six months from now. So, this could be our last few days together. Maybe. Maybe not if you make a choice. But I am not here to impose my proposal…hmmm…I am only here to make things straight that I should've done earlier. Not telling Naads would be the biggest fraud and Nicole, I am the one who catches them; I can't be one of them! This act doesn't reflect well on our love.'

'We've no love.'

'Agreed. You don't. I do. Now let's talk sense.'

'See you.'

As he took the stairs, he returned, and involuntarily kissed Nicola. And even she didn't resist. 'You don't have to create a conflict. It could be solved,' said Scott and left. It was no less than 30 minutes when she found Nayantara at her doorstep. Astounded as she was and as much, she was happy to meet Nayantara after a long time. How could she not be happier as her life had turned out to be a glorious stretch of salvation by reading her poems. She had evolved, turned a little seasoned and all she had to be thankful to was Nayantara.

'Nayantara! I am glad to see you!' as she said, she embraced her.

On seeing her joyous and effervescent, I didn't consider interjecting her state of being. And neither did I want to pause her flow of emotions. So, what if she'd messed up? She is just 27, a widow with a child, who's just trying to make her ends meet, and recurrently pours her out to anyone who sees to be a promise of love.

'It's alright to be playful, to just be oneself, to play stupid, restless, be impulsive, and also mellow down, to feel jumpy and yet try to feel great about everything running around; to want, to desire, to feel the thrill, to be a part of it, to be real. 'Yes, it's judicious to be sorted but exhilarating to be real! And Nicole, you are the perfectly imperfect- the true real! And I know about you and Scott!'

Nicola thudded onto the floor. She was ashamed, and she couldn't look at Nayantara into her eyes. Her remorseful body wouldn't respond to the stimuli.

I bent down and held her closely. 'It's alright for a girl to be unfeigned and embrace the truth. And let me not give you a lecture on morals or realizations, either on misdeeds or intoxicated actions. These are nothing but heavy concepts built by men from generations after generations; to put gutsy, vibrant people like you chained and controlled. To drill a hole in your continuous space where love is felt by intimacy, and intimacy by the tangible living beings. There's no ascendance of the order of love- do what suits you, what makes you free…just don't be pained or chained. I am no judge and neither do I want to be one. Not at this stage of my life! So, get up and live your life. It's for once and meant for people who are thrilled to take a chance.'

I called up Scott, explaining that he was required here, with Nicole.

'Who told you, Nayantara?'

'Who else but Mrs Patrick! She was embarrassed, and I was upset too! But no sooner I realized that this phenomenon called life will poof in the air suddenly. And in these tumultuous complexities which are created by us, we'll lose out on living its gorgeous moments.'

'No words would be enough fulfilment to thank your greatness! I am sorry that it had to be Scott.'

'If it had to be Scott, then what for the apology, huh?'

'I have a surprise for you and that's the main reason for my visit. Allow me, please.'

As Nayantara was tearing off the envelope, Nicola asked her to stop and hold on for some more time. She handed her the manuscript, bound in spirals and typed in free-hand. It called out- 'Sonnets to Paradise.'

'But I've not written any poem of that title!'

'If you've not, please do me a favour… pen it.'

I stepped out of Mrs Patrick's house, carrying my thickened manuscript which was made-over intrinsically by Nicola and also the envelope which as per her contained a surprise. I was pleased by her involvement in my manuscript and her belief in me to write the title as something that has not struck me ever. 'What could I pen with a poem that titles itself it be 'Sonnets to Paradise', huh!' I kept asking myself on my way back.

'Where are your friends?'

'They'll be here in an hour. They will taste your delicacies.'

Mrs Patrick was helping my father re-arrange the library, and I found a heap of books lying all over the study. I just said, 'thank you' to her and disappeared from the confusion lying around.

Without finding my space, I left for the small house lawn. Discovering peace, I opened the letter, and it had the header of Writers & Poets! I looked up, couldn't find my stars shining brightly, yet could view the weather changing from dark-clouds to a whimpering ray of the golden crease. 'No words would be enough to thank you, Nicole.' I murmured on getting sentimental.

Later that night, after a sumptuous, joyful feast with extravaganza, I re-read the contract letter. In the same night, Nicola smiled with Adrian and her mother with no pauses and wails; and she called up Scott to say, 'I'll wait for you to be back from Spain.'

Holding the manuscript that was arranged by Nicola, I opened the study drawer and saw old pictures of Goa. Jojo, Reena, and me. I smiled too and then found the only picture that I had clicked with Ronnie, many years back in London. It was dated 2007, an office get-together…I shuffled through my phone yet again and checked the chat history where Rubail had sent me his number.

'Hi, How time flies by--Nayantara.'

And the next morning, I was able to pen something as odd yet truthful to the title….

Sonnets to Paradise

Zen in my attribute
Peace on my mind,

No thrill may disrupt it
No perverse thought at my hind,

Belonging to the Supernova change
My concepts have carved a dime,

Come, sit next to me
So that your heart may even hum a rhyme,

Where music throngs and strings chime
Where the cuckoo sings on the coniferous pines
O, gentleman! O ladies, you are welcomed
To knock at the Gates of my Paradise!

If the gates are closed, worry not you
As day will emerge at the backyard of the moon,
Bring the harp, strike the doom
As you shall perpetually be welcomed
To enter the Gates of my Paradise!

Scribbling this…Scrapping that
As my poem had a jumpy start
Never mind the uneven history
As even the forest sometimes turns into a mystery

And this is where the saga begins as it ends
In praise, in satire to my Sonnets to Paradise

About the Author

Nidra Naik is an Indian novelist and a poet.

She is the author of 'The Bhubaneswar Times' and 'A Lot Like Love & Other Short Stories', both of which are works of fiction. Her musings for writing poems have been immense, so much that few of her poems have been published in anthologies of 'Out of the Woods' and 'Moonlight'.

She comes from a family of writers, musicians, and actors, however, with a humble upbringing and an intense value system. She has spent most of her childhood in her hometown, Cuttack, which is a quaint little town in the coastal belt of Odisha.

After she graduated from the renowned Ravenshaw University, with a Bachelor's degree in Commerce (management honours distinction), she decided to see the world around and headed to New Delhi for an MBA in marketing at the esteemed management college of IILM. Ironically, none in her family or immediate family had pursued business studies! It was in New Delhi that she got a streak of thought of becoming a writer and was eventually getting aware of her interests and likes.

Returning to Bhubaneswar, while having taken a job, she penned her first novel. And her most inspirational muse for the book had been none other than her then beau, now husband, who she got married to later.

These days, she writes quotes by the hashtag of #ThinkingNidra, which can be extensively found on her Instagram handle. Nidra is also getting trained in Hindustani classical music as she has a passion for music too.

She's also appeared in many interviews on bloggers' website, publishers' author corners, Bhubaneswar-Radio, Odia-TV channel, English, Odia & Bengali newspapers regarding her work.

She currently works & lives in Hyderabad with her husband and two pet dogs. Being an ardent lover of animals & nature, she spends her free hours reducing carbon/water prints, petting animals, endorsing cruelty-free products, supporting animal organizations, old age organizations, and encouraging her friends and relatives to do so.